TREATS FOR LUCIA
HOLIDAY DADDY DOMS
BOOK THREE

RAISA GREYWOOD

Cover art by Allysa Hart.
Editing provided by Amy Briggs.

Ebook ISBN: 978-1-952596-03-2
Print ISBN: 978-1-952596-04-9

PROLOGUE

"*I* can't believe you brought me here, Serena. And for a pagan celebration, no less."

Serena rolled her eyes. Of all the people with whom she could have shared her favorite holiday, Gabriel didn't even make the top hundred. Lucifer would have been a much better escort for Saints and Sinners' annual Halloween Masquerade, but he wasn't talking to her at the moment.

One of these days, he'd figure out not everyone would kneel to him just because he was the devil. Although he was an excellent conversationalist and his naughty smiles made her lady bits flutter, it would be a cold day in… well, Hell before she bent a

1

knee for an arrogant fallen angel with a superiority complex.

"Lighten up. It's a party," she finally said. "I told you I'd be taking guardianship of Lucia. You're the one who decided to come along to make sure I did it right."

As if she hadn't been a guardian of sorts for most of her adult life. *Asshole*.

Straightening his robe, Gabriel snorted and averted his gaze from a young lady trussed in a suspension harness. Her blissed-out expression made Serena smile. Irritating archangel in tow, she made her way across the dungeon to the dais where Lucia reigned over the celebration.

Sparkling with crystals, a Venetian mask covered Lucia's gorgeous eyes, and her red-painted lips were flat and unsmiling. Her white leather corset dress was the perfect adornment for her lush figure, and curly sable hair trailed in spirals to her waist. On her graceful feet, she wore the black Louboutin stilettos Serena had given her for their last Christmas together.

"Still so beautiful," Serena murmured. "You shouldn't be sad anymore, baby doll."

"Come to a decision so we can leave," Gabriel

snapped. "This is a den of iniquity, and if the other angels hear I came to this place—"

"Hush and open your eyes. Do you see people hurting each other? Are they unkind? Are they committing cardinal sins?"

"They're all hurting each other. That man is whipping another."

"And he loves every minute of it." Serena focused on Ryan Sarver, one of her toys from before, and pursed her lips in thought. He and his best friend, Mitchell Sakurai, usually played together, but Mitchell was in Afghanistan. An itch of premonition tickled the base of her spine, and she made a note to check on him. For now, Lucia needed her attention.

Still busy with his sub, Ryan's mask and jacket laid on a bench off to the side and his tie hung loosely around his neck. His dark hair was disheveled, making him look like a very sexy rogue. The sleeves of his dress shirt were rolled up to reveal thick forearms, corded with exertion as he stroked the man with a single-tail whip. Serena nodded in approval. He'd been practicing.

Le sigh. Her baby boy was all grown up and doing demo scenes of his own. If she hadn't kicked off this mortal coil so abruptly, she could have watched

Ryan and Mitchell both find submissives. They reminded her so much of Kaden and Tennyson, both of whom were rusticating in Vermont with their new wives. Tennyson was even soon to be the father of two baby girls. Well, four if one counted Chelsea and their dog Princess.

"This place is filled with drugs and alcohol," Gabriel retorted, interrupting her reverie. "Look at that woman. She can barely walk."

Bullshit. No intoxicating substances of any kind were permitted in Saints and Sinners. Just having it in the building was enough for a member to earn a lifetime ban. Narrowing her eyes, Serena followed Gabriel's accusing finger, then relaxed.

"The lucky girl is floating through subspace. She'll be…" The woman's dom wrapped her trembling body in a blanket and carried her to a couch. A club submissive brought water and a tray of snacks, then hurried away, leaving them alone. "She'll be perfectly fine."

"Sounds dangerous," Gabriel muttered. "She's on something."

"Just the endorphins your god gave her to make her feel good. Stop being such a judgmental ass and look at them."

Thankfully, he lapsed into a huffy silence and obeyed, his eyes turning thoughtful when the dom hummed a soft lullaby to his drowsy lady. She didn't have long to wait for the inevitable questions.

"Why is he coddling her after she displeased him?"

Gabriel truly didn't get it and Serena wondered why she cared. "What makes you think she did something wrong?"

"Well, he beat her with a leather strap. It must have been punishment."

"Or maybe it's part of their dynamic and something they both enjoy," she countered.

"How do you know?"

"Because I introduced them to each other." Serena went silent for a moment, then added, "Now, be quiet. I'm working."

After spending several months studying past guardians, she had a decent grasp of what would be required of her. Keep her charges safe and help them find true love. Much to Gabriel's disgust, she focused her attention on Edith Barber, the guardian angel who had brought Tennyson and Chelsea together. Edith had a certain *savoir vivre* she admired—especially since it annoyed Gabriel.

Edith thrived on serendipity and chaos. If two people were in close proximity, she could tell whether they'd suit each other and didn't waste her time if there wasn't chemistry.

Serena took another look at Ryan. She might not have Edith's magic, but she wasn't blind. Her former toy wasn't hanging around for his health. Judging by the way his gaze kept returning to Lucia, he was there for her.

Her work was done. Serena rubbed her hands together and smirked. Even if Lucia wasn't quite ready to embrace the idea of finding a partner, she should have happiness. It was no stretch to imagine her with Ryan, and they'd played together under Serena's guidance in the past. Lucia was always a baby dom's first. She was sufficiently dominant to make sure they got it right, but was submissive enough to melt even the most dedicated sadist.

Of all the people Serena could have chosen, Ryan would be the best fit for her sad baby doll. He had the right mix of qualities to be just what she needed —as long as Lucia opened up enough to let him.

In fact, he would probably be better at it than Serena had been.

Ignoring Gabriel's squawks of disapproval, she

crossed the dungeon to the dais and resisted the urge to lay a hand on Lucia's shoulder. She rarely bothered to follow rules unless they were her own, but touch was strictly forbidden. It would make her visible to the human she was assigned to protect. No good would come of that foolishness.

Picking up her glass, Lucia took a deep drink of what looked like cranberry juice over ice. Yet it was pale and watery as if…

Creeping closer, Serena inhaled the sharp bite of vodka. Disappointment warred with sadness and she sighed softly. Lucia knew better than to drink in Saints and Sinners. Even a founding member, as Lucia was, wasn't above the rules. What was she thinking? Thank goodness she wasn't actually playing tonight. At least she had enough sense to stay seated.

"Oh, baby doll, you're in for it now," Serena murmured, waving a hand to switch Lucia's glass with Ryan's water. Affecting inanimate objects with angelic power to encourage specific behavior was well within her abilities, as long as she didn't directly guide their choices.

Without looking, Ryan picked it up and took a drink, then put a hand over his mouth and coughed.

His eyes narrowing, he turned to face Lucia, pinning her with a glare promising retribution.

Lucia paled and bit her lip, but lifted her chin in defiance and stood to leave. He was on her in a flash and returned her to her seat, smoothly handcuffing her wrist to the chair before he made sure his partner for the scene had sufficient aftercare.

She was in good hands. Serena understood grief, but alcohol wasn't going to solve Lucia's problems. Even if things didn't work out with Ryan, he'd snap her out of those self-destructive behaviors.

"You'll be happy to know we're done here," she finally said to Gabriel, watching Ryan escort Lucia from the club.

"You didn't do anything. You should follow—"

"I did enough," she retorted. "It's not my job to hold their hands. You said yourself I can only guide people, and that's just what I did."

Grunting, he gave her a suspicious look. "How? You can't possibly expect switching their glasses to work. What if he whips her like he did to that man?"

"She'd have it coming for bringing alcohol into Saints and Sinners." When Gabriel sputtered, Serena held up a hand. "Not one word. You don't get to impose your judgment on my charges. We've already had this discussion and I don't care to repeat myself."

"You're worse than Edith," he muttered, scowling.

"Thank you. Now, if you'll excuse me, I'm going to see Lucifer. He's better company than you are."

With luck, she'd be able to tease him into talking to her again. Otherwise, life as an angel was going to be deadly boring.

CHAPTER 1

*T*oo furious to speak, Ryan kept silent. The sidewalk outside Saints and Sinners was no place to flip up Lucia's dress and blister her backside for drinking in the club. He needed to calm down before he risked saying a word.

Lucia needed a come to Jesus moment before she imploded. Between missing work and bringing alcohol to the club, she was spiraling down and this was the absolute last thing he was going to tolerate.

Everyone missed Serena, and Lucia had been her partner for almost five years. A person didn't lose someone that close to them without grieving, and Serena's heart attack had been so sudden and unexpected, nobody had time to prepare. Or to say goodbye.

Tears misted his vision as he frog-marched her to his car, but he blinked them back before they fell. He had to focus on Lucia. No one could wipe away her heartbreak, but she had to realize people cared enough not to let her destroy her life.

"Where are you taking me? I want to go home."

"That might be the first smart decision you've made all night," he muttered. "I'm taking you home so we can have a little chat."

"I don't want to talk." She yanked her arms free and strode in the opposite direction. "Go away."

He stepped in front of her, then leaned close. "You have a choice, Lucia. You can let me drive you home, or I'll go back inside and tell the manager you were drinking."

Straightening, she tried to look down her nose at him. Quite a feat for a woman almost a foot shorter than his six feet, three inches. "Go ahead. They won't believe you."

"You know the rules, little girl. I tasted your drink. It was vodka with enough cranberry juice to give it a little color. Think you'll pass the breathalyzer?"

Flushing, she held her ground, but Ryan didn't miss the way her eyes darted around, looking to see if someone heard. "Fine," she snapped, glaring at him. "What do you want?"

"As I said, I'm taking you home. We'll discuss what happens after that when we get there."

"And if I refuse?"

"Make a good choice, honey." He opened the front passenger door and stepped back so she could get in. "Talk with me or get a lifetime ban from Saints and Sinners."

"Fine!" She threw up her hands and stalked back, then climbed in, crossing her arms over her chest. Her huffy silence spoke louder than anything she might have said.

He tried not to be distracted by the way her position plumped her breasts up above the cups of her corset. Lucia wasn't in any danger, but her ass was going to be. He'd never know how he managed to resist the urge to turn her over his knee for the whole twenty-minute drive to her Brooklyn brownstone. Luckily, he managed to snag the unicorn of parking spots less than a block away.

Keeping a firm hold on her arm, Ryan walked her up the stone steps to her front door. He wouldn't put it past her to attempt an escape. To her credit, she didn't protest when he took her keys and opened the door, then urged her inside, leaving their coats on the tree in the corner.

Heels clicking on the polished parquet flooring, she walked across the elegant foyer to the sitting room, turning on lights as she went. "You've brought me home," she finally said, retrieving a bottle and glass from the sideboard across from the fireplace. She ignored him when he followed her. "Say what you have to say and get out."

"That's not how this works," he said softly, tugging the bottle from her grasp before she could pour. "How much did you have to drink?"

"Less than I wanted to. I only got a few sips before you took my drink away." Giving him a push, she reached for the bottle.

Instead of giving it to her, he marched into the kitchen and poured it out, ignoring her screeches. "Lucia, I know you're a domme in your own right, but you're acting like a spoiled brat."

"And? What do you care?"

"I care for you too much to allow you to self-destruct, so you're going to pull up your dress and lay yourself over my lap for a spanking."

"Or what?" she challenged, furious tears welling in her eyes.

"Or I leave and call the club manager to have you

banned. I'm not going to force you, but you will choose one or the other."

Lucia might be an accomplished domme, but she submitted just as beautifully for the right person. Watching her with Serena during their demos had been gorgeous, and she'd been an amazing submissive. Ryan wasn't sure he could be what she needed, but he had to make her see the path she was determined to follow wasn't in her best interest. Then again, Lucia had submitted to him in the past. Regardless of Serena's wishes, she'd have refused if he hadn't had the chops to carry it off.

In the months since Serena's untimely passing, Lucia had become morose and distant. He'd hoped to cheer her up and make her remember how much fun Saints and Sinners could be, so he selected a young man for a demo scene, knowing Lucia would love watching him work. With luck, she'd have chosen a partner, either a dominant or a submissive, and...

Well, best laid plans and all that.

Instead of enjoying the festivities, she'd risked losing everything for a glass of vodka. He stalked toward her, making her blink and take a step back.

"Make your choice, sweetheart," he said softly, his

voice deepening into the husky growl designed to make even the strongest sub melt into a puddle.

"I don't consent," she retorted. "Go fuck yourself."

"Okay." Biting back his disappointment, Ryan strode to the foyer for his coat. "Best wishes to you. I'm afraid I won't be seeing you at Saints and Sinners anymore, but I'm sure you'll be fine on your own."

As much as it pained him, he had to make a stand and leave. Without her consent, he wasn't going to do shit. The worst thing he could do would be to fail in his follow up. Sadly, it would mean letting her go. It went against everything he believed to let a friend suffer by herself, and he couldn't help but think Serena would have done better. She'd have found the right thing to say.

A cool fall breeze wafted in when he opened the door, and he sighed before putting on his jacket.

"Wait."

He turned when she laid her hand on his shoulder, but kept his face impassive. "Why? You already said you weren't willing to talk or take the correction you need, and you've asked me to leave."

She chewed her lower lip, making it plump and swell. "What happens if I say yes?"

"You go over my knee for a sound spanking, then

I'll make you some hot chocolate and put you to bed after our talk."

Resisting the urge to pull her lip from between her teeth, Ryan waited her out. Finally, she nodded.

"All right, but no more than five."

Arching a brow, he nodded. "Fair enough. Go get your hairbrush. And I don't mean the one in your bathroom. Get the one from the playroom."

Her eyes widened. "But you said—"

"I said you'd be getting a spanking. I didn't say I'd use my hand. You have sixty seconds."

Shoes flying off her feet, she squeaked and disappeared down the stairs.

Thank fuck.

Belatedly, he remembered to check his watch for the time, but it wasn't necessary. She raced up the stairs as quickly as she'd gone down, carrying a wide wooden paddle the size and shape of an old-fashioned brush.

He took the paddle, then led her to the couch and sat down. "Over my knee, baby girl."

"Fine. Let's get this over with."

Ryan hid a chuckle. Ballsy to the very end. Gingerly, she knelt on the couch next to him and slowly lowered her torso over his lap.

Repositioning her so her butt was right where he

17

wanted it, he stroked her plump backside, then tugged the leather skirt up, baring surprisingly modest lacy white panties. She'd get to keep those. It wasn't as if the flimsy silk was any barrier to a wooden paddle.

"You don't have to count," he murmured, his voice deeper and huskier than he intended. This was a punishment, so he didn't bother with a warmup.

Lifting his arm, Ryan brought the paddle down on the lower curve of her ass. She hissed, her feet coming up off the couch. He gave her a moment to settle down, then spanked her in earnest, peppering her bottom with firm slaps of the paddle.

"Ouch! That's more than five!" She kicked again and he delivered a harder swat to the crease between her buttocks and thighs, making her yell out a curse.

"Careful, baby girl. Do you want me to add to your punishment?"

"You agreed to five!"

"I did," he replied, spanking her again, catching the other side of her ass. "But you didn't say what we were counting. I chose five minutes."

"You son of a..." Gritting her teeth, she spat the words between spanks. "I hate you."

Ryan tugged her panties down to reveal her nicely reddened backside, then delivered several harder spanks to her tender sit spot, making her howl. When she tried to cover her ass with her hands, he grabbed her wrists and pinned them behind her back.

"You can hate me all you want," he said calmly, delivering another flurry of swats to her bottom. "As long as you stop trying to ruin your own life."

"Please." Tears thickened her voice and she coughed to clear her throat. "I just…"

She burst into noisy sobs. Finally. Crossing his fingers, he prayed he'd find the right way to help Lucia. He settled her in his lap and held her while she cried her eyes out.

"Good girl," he murmured, stroking her hair. "It's going to be okay."

"Liar." She shivered. "I miss her so much."

This was a punishment, so Ryan wasn't going to rub the sting from her backside. Instead, he dropped a kiss on her temple, then dragged a fleece blanket over her. "I do too, baby girl. Serena was one of a kind."

"What do I do now?" She sat up and he gave her a handkerchief to wipe her face. "I'm just… lost, I guess."

"You can't keep trying to self-destruct," he said gently, biting back the lecture she probably deserved. Lucia didn't need orders or ultimatums. She needed understanding and time to work through her grief. "I'm your friend, and I want to help you."

"You were going to leave," she retorted.

"You told me to. I wasn't going to stay without your consent."

A wry smile crossed her lips and she rested her head on his shoulder. "Serena taught you way too well."

Holding Lucia felt good, and he resisted the urge to kiss her. "But we're still going to talk. You can't keep doing this shit. You've lost weight, and I'm worried about you."

She shifted in his arms, then stared at the side-board. "I'm… Yeah, I was about to say I'm fine, but I'm not. It isn't your problem." Wriggling free, she sat up and perched on the edge of the couch. "You need to find a sub of your own instead of worrying about me, but I appreciate the thought."

Ryan caught her before she could get up, then tucked her back into his lap. "Baby girl, you can do better than that."

LUCIA'S HEAD ached from crying and she wanted a drink. She'd more than earned a punishment, but her butt still ached. At least Ryan hadn't ordered corner time. That would have undone her completely, and she'd already come too close to revealing her secrets.

She hadn't even wanted to go out tonight, but a founding member of Saints and Sinners didn't bail on the Halloween Masquerade without good reason, and she'd already missed too many events as it was.

Being with Ryan was way too comfortable. He might have been Serena's student, but he'd developed more than enough dominant presence to make Lucia's inner sub sit up and take notice. Any woman would be thrilled to be in the arms of one of the hottest doms in New York. What was wrong with her? And why the hell had she let him see her cry? She wished she could have blamed it on booze, but she hadn't lied about being sober. She hadn't gotten more than a few sips of vodka before Ryan took the drink away.

Except for planned exercises for baby doms like Ryan and his best friend Mitchell, Lucia hadn't truly submitted to anyone in years. She wanted to, but... No. It wasn't worth the risk.

Serena had been safe, and gave Lucia what she

needed without making her feel less about herself. They'd never been lovers though, despite what everyone thought. Ryan didn't know the real Lucia or the true nature of the relationship she and Serena had shared.

He saw the public persona she presented. She kept herself hidden from everyone but Serena. If he knew what she needed... She didn't delude herself into thinking he'd be willing to spend one more second with her, and he certainly wouldn't be interested in what she truly craved.

In a valiant attempt to ignore the spare bottle under the sideboard, Lucia gave him her best cheerful smile, hoping it didn't look like a death rictus. "I'll be fine," she said, trying to extricate herself from his octopus arms. "Go home, and I promise we'll get together for lunch next week."

Ryan simply stared at her, and God help her, Lucia's heart fell and soared at the same time. "No, I don't think so, baby girl," he said softly, his deep, throaty dom voice making her want to collapse at his feet.

"What do you mean, no?" Serena had always called her baby doll, and it was close enough to make tears well again. Yet at the same time, her core spasmed and clenched with arousal. She wanted to give in so badly, but the cost would be too high.

He stood, towering over her, and held out a hand. "Stand up."

She was on her feet before she recognized what she was doing. Damn it. In an effort to hide how quickly she'd obeyed, Lucia walked to the fireplace and reached for the switch to turn on the gas logs.

Ryan covered her hand with a massive paw, stopping her. "Are you cold?"

"No, I—"

"Good. Turn around." His large hands firm on her shoulders, he turned her until her back was to him, then unlaced her corset.

Lucia let out a relieved moan as the tight garment fell open. As much as she liked wearing corsets, taking them off was a pleasure all its own. "Thanks," she murmured, attempting to step away from his enticing warmth.

"You're welcome." He didn't let her go right away, but eventually dropped his hands to his sides. "Go change. I'll make some hot chocolate and we'll talk."

Thankful for the chance to escape, she nodded and went upstairs. As it had been for months, the door to Serena's bedroom remained steadfastly closed. She hadn't even let the cleaning lady in there.

Going into her own room, Lucia changed into leggings and a battered college sweatshirt before hanging her party clothes in the closet. She liked Ryan. He was sexy as hell, and one of the best doms she knew, but she couldn't ask him to be what she needed. Even if they had a relationship beyond friendship, it would be too much.

Pushing the thought away, Lucia washed up and put her hair into a messy bun, then went back downstairs, hoping she didn't look like a zombie. She could fake cheerfulness well enough to get him out of her house, then go back to her plans for the evening.

Drink until you cry yourself to sleep? Smart.

Ugh. Lucia's inner bitch voice sounded exactly like Serena when she scolded her.

Inhaling the scent of warm chocolate with vanilla, she walked into the kitchen, then stopped short. Ryan was… cooking. With a saucepan and the stove.

"What are you doing?"

"Making hot cocoa. You only had dry mix," he replied, pulling a measuring cup full of melted chocolate from the microwave above the stove. "I dug into your stash of good candy, there was cream and milk in the fridge, and you had sugar in the pantry."

Damn, he was hot. His tie hung loose around his neck and his sleeves were rolled up, but his shirt was still tucked in, revealing his tight backside in snug trousers.

She could see herself becoming connected to Ryan very easily, which was also very bad. She was a hot mess, and still grieved her best friend. He'd have no interest in her baggage, and he didn't deserve to have her dump it on him.

He was right though. Lucia was going off the deep end. She was one missed deadline away from losing her job. She'd risked her membership to Saints and Sinners. She knew all that, but couldn't seem to stop herself. Everything was just too much to handle without Serena by her side. What she wouldn't give for one more discussion with her. Of course, it would have ended up with her over Serena's lap getting her butt blistered. Even though they'd never been lovers, Serena didn't hesitate to deliver a spanking when Lucia needed it.

Lucia couldn't even dominate another sub. How could she when she could barely control herself?

Whisking slowly, he dribbled chocolate into the saucepan of hot milk, then added a pinch of salt and more vanilla. It smelled so good. Instead of moaning in pleasure, she got mugs from the cupboard.

"Thanks," he said, taking the mugs from her. Without spilling a drop, he divided the mixture between them, then carried them to the kitchen table. "Have a seat, baby girl. It's time for our chat."

CHAPTER 2

*L*ucia cradled her mug in small hands, then took a sip. "Delicious," she murmured, looking down at the table. "Where did you learn to make this?"

"YouTube. Care to tell me why you decided to risk losing your membership to Saints and Sinners?"

Her eyes darted to his face, then she looked away. "Not really, no."

Disappointment warred with anger, making Ryan take a deep breath before he put her over his knee again. Something was going on in her head, and he needed to find out what it was before he went further. She might not call him back if she threw him out again. "All right. Let's rephrase the question. Do you want to give up your membership?"

"Sometimes…" She shook her head. "Yeah. Most of the time, I do."

"Did you consider a leave of absence instead of getting yourself banned?"

"Harsh." She took another sip of cocoa.

Ryan liked giving her something she enjoyed. She still looked sad and upset, but at least she wasn't giving the bar those not-so-secretive glances anymore. He especially liked watching her fidget on the hardwood kitchen chair.

"It's true though." He took her hand, then kissed her fingertips. "What do you need, baby girl? What can I do to help you?"

"Nothing. I'll be fine. Would it make you happy if I suspend my membership for a few months?"

"We're talking about what will make *you* happy," he countered. "Not me."

She sighed and shook her head. "I have no idea what will make me happy. I thought going to the club would help, but it just made things worse." Lifting the mug to her lips, she finished her drink. "Maybe I should get out of town for a few weeks."

"What about your job?"

"Yeah, I know." Grimacing, she grunted sourly.

"I've already been told I'd be fired if I miss any more work, so that idea will have to wait until after the holidays."

"Wise decision," he murmured. "I know Serena left you taken care of, but I don't want to see you lose your livelihood."

A sweet smile danced across her face before disappearing. "Yeah, she left me this house, and enough to keep it up for a while. She was always trying to take care of me, just like a good m—" She coughed, then continued. "Anyway, the cocoa was great. Thanks for making it."

When her eyes drooped and she yawned, he chose not to press her for what she'd almost said. Instead, he carried their mugs to the sink, then helped her up. "It's time for little girls to go to bed," he murmured, wrapping an arm around her waist.

"I'm fine," she replied, stepping out of his embrace. "I don't need someone to tuck me in, so you can go. I promise, I'll call you next week."

A sigh of irritation almost escaped and he shook his head. "I'm staying the night on your couch, baby girl."

She rolled her eyes and huffed. "Seriously, no. Go home."

"Do you want another spanking?"

"What? No, I—"

"You keep looking at your liquor stash, and I'm not going to let you drink yourself to sleep."

"Rude!"

"Maybe. Count yourself lucky I won't be tying you down to make sure you stay put." Her expression darkened, and Ryan held up a hand to stop whatever she'd been about to say. "You can go to bed on your own, or I can put you there. Choose wisely."

"Fine!" Without another word, she whirled around and stomped up the stairs. A door slammed a second later, making him smile.

Lucia was bratting for all she was worth, which was very unusual for her. Small doses were fun, but not something he'd tolerate for long—even if her little tantrums were too cute for words. She might be dominant with most people, but he wondered how often and in what context she'd submitted to Serena.

If he didn't know better, he'd say she was acting out like a neglected little. That was silly though. It just didn't fit. Letting out a sigh, he returned to the kitchen and cleaned up, then found bedding in the beautifully carved blanket chest he and Mitchell had fetched from the artist, Chelsea Barber, in Vermont. Serena had been so excited about it, but she'd passed away before they got back to New York.

Stripping down to his T-shirt and boxer briefs, Ryan washed up in the powder room, then stretched out on the surprisingly comfortable couch and closed his eyes.

A noise woke him, and it took a few seconds to orient himself to his location and the sound. Sitting up, he slid his legs into his trousers, then crept up the stairs, following the faint crying. He hadn't seen Serena and Lucia's private space before. There were four doors, one of which was closed.

Opening it, he frowned. It was a bedroom, tidy, but smelling of dust and disuse. He crept inside and peeked into the closet, gasping when he found Serena's familiar fetish wear. He saw nothing he thought might be Lucia's, meaning she didn't sleep in the neatly made double sleigh bed.

Hadn't they been a couple? Ryan couldn't understand why they wouldn't have been sharing a room. The mechanics of their relationship were none of his business, but he was very curious.

He crept out, shutting the door with a quiet click, then crossed the hall to the other bedroom. Peeking inside, Ryan held back a gasp at the sight of Lucia curled up in a twin canopy bed with pink curtains and bedding. The room was filled with toys, stuffed animals, and dolls, and a table in the corner was laden with art supplies. Posters of unicorns and teddy bears covered the walls.

A small rainbow-colored cat was on the floor next to the bed, looking like it had fallen. Moving silently, he picked it up and tucked it into her arms. Thankfully, she stopped crying and settled back into sleep, clutching the toy to her chest.

"Damn," he murmured, creeping down the stairs. "No wonder."

Lucia *was* a little. How had he never known that? It changed everything. A little without a mommy or daddy was a catastrophe. And to lose Serena so suddenly... Poor baby girl. Ryan's chest ached with sympathy.

Judging by the stuff in her bedroom, he estimated her little's age to be around six or seven. It was frankly amazing she'd managed to hold her shit together as well as she had for so long. It also explained the stale dinosaur marshmallows he'd found in her pantry.

He shouldn't have spanked her without knowing the whole story, but who could have guessed? Lucia Alvarez had been one of the most popular pro dommes in the city. Although she was widely known as a switch, no one would have dreamed she'd be a little.

She was such a dichotomy, yet he relished the challenge she presented. It didn't hurt she was fucking gorgeous, but that wasn't what attracted him. As a domme, she was scorching. As a little, she made him want to take care of her. And when she was a grownup submissive, he wanted to do all manner of dirty, dirty things to her beautifully curved body.

Being allowed to watch her scene with a submissive. Putting her on the cross for some impact play afterwards. Making her teddy bear pancakes with chocolate chips and whipped cream in the morning before letting her play with her toys... Ryan couldn't have put a more perfect woman together if he'd built her out of Legos.

He tried to erase the predatory grin from his face and sent Ebony, his PA, an email canceling his appointments for the rest of the month. As a freelance programmer, Ryan didn't have a set schedule, so he'd be able to devote most of his time to giving Lucia what she needed. There were a few projects he couldn't ignore, but he'd deal with them while she was at work.

Wishing he had his laptop, Ryan used his phone

to research activities that would appeal to a closeted baby girl. There was a vibrant little's group at Saints and Sinners, but he was sure she wouldn't talk to them. He'd be on his own with the small amount of knowledge he had regarding the care and feeding of a healthy little.

Scanning through the offerings, he paused at the perfect idea. She didn't know it yet, but Lucia was going to get a Halloween worth remembering.

Crossing his fingers, he prayed he didn't make things worse. Her attitude, and the fact that she'd so firmly shut her little down, meant he'd have his work cut out for him.

"WHAT DO YOU THINK, Kitty? Is he still downstairs?"

Lucia curled up with Princess Rainbow Kitty, needing just a few more minutes to herself before she took a chance and went downstairs. She hadn't heard him moving around yet and crossed her fingers, hoping he was already gone.

As much as she wanted to stay in her room and play, she wanted coffee more than she wanted her coloring books and toys. Clutching the toy to her chest, she stretched and got up.

Maybe it was because of Ryan's spanking, but she'd slept surprisingly well. Although her butt was still sore, she'd needed it. She had been very naughty. Acting out was never a good choice, but with no one left to punish her for bad behavior, she just... did it.

Still, Lucia's little was content for the moment, and she was... Maybe not content, but at least she wasn't in the kitchen mixing up a pitcher of screwdrivers for breakfast.

"Okay," she murmured. "Ryan is gone, so coffee."

The minute her foot touched the bottom stair, she smelled a faint whiff of bacon and maple syrup.

She crept to the kitchen, peeking around the edge of the wall dividing it from the rest of the house. Standing at the stove over a pair of skillets, Ryan wore nothing but a pair of boxer briefs and an apron.

Holy mother of... *Dayum.* Her mouth watered, both for the food, and for the incredibly gorgeous man plating breakfast.

Fuck. She couldn't decide whether to curl in his lap with Kitty or get on her knees to suck his cock. It wouldn't have been a first for her either. He had an awesome dick, thick and sweet, with perfect veins she wanted to trace with her tongue.

35

Okay, no. Not the time. Not the place, and definitely not the man.

"Good morning," he said, making Lucia jump. "Ready for breakfast, baby girl?"

"I…" Swallowing hard, she made a beeline for the Keurig. "Why are you still here?"

"After breakfast, I have a surprise for you," he replied, setting a plate on the table. "Have a seat. I already have your coffee made."

Oh, God, he'd filled her favorite unicorn mug with the dark roast Jamaican blend she preferred.

"Just the coffee, thanks." She reached for the cup, but he held it out of reach.

"Sit down, Lucia."

Her butt hit the seat faster than she'd have liked. He pushed every one of her buttons. Nearly naked man waiting on her domme, the sexy, sultry authoritative voice giving her submissive chills, and…

God help her, pancakes shaped like teddy bears with chocolate chips and whipped cream.

Realizing he'd somehow learned her secret, she jerked away and jumped out of her chair. Her stomach heaved and she swallowed hard before she threw up. She should have known better than to allow him to stay. What had she been thinking to leave herself so vulnerable? He was going to tell everyone, and… Tears welled and she blinked them back furiously.

"How dare you?" Still holding Kitty in her arms, Lucia strode to the couch and tossed his clothes at him. "Get out."

"Lucia, it's okay." Ryan held his hands out and walked to her, still wearing the apron. "It's your secret to keep. I won't tell anyone, but you need to listen to me."

"No, I really don't," she snapped. "I asked you to leave."

"Not until you hear what I have to say."

Darting forward, he caught her in his arms and carried her to the couch, ignoring her angry curses. Before she knew it, she was curled up on his lap, holding Kitty, just like she used to sit with Serena. Her head ached with the force of tears she refused to let fall.

"Just go away." She couldn't do this. Any minute he would tell her how no one would ever want her, and that she was sick for pretending to be a kid.

"Serena was your mommy, wasn't she? You weren't a couple at all," he said when she gave up trying to get away.

She nodded miserably and buried her face in Kitty's soft fur, waiting for his judgment.

Instead of letting her go, he tightened his arms around her. "Oh, sweetheart, being a little is nothing to be ashamed of. Why didn't you want me to know?"

A burden shared is a burden lessened, baby doll.

Stupid inner voice. Letting out a sigh, Lucia decided she might as well just tell him. Ryan was the stubbornest man she'd ever met, and he wasn't likely to give up until she spilled all her secrets. Strangely enough, she trusted him enough to keep them.

"Once upon a time, there was a stupid little girl who got married right out of high school to an older dominant man," she finally said. Speaking about herself in the third person seemed to make it easier. "Things were perfect until the day the girl decided he loved her enough to be her daddy and let her little come out."

"Oh, honey." His arms tightened around her and she choked back another sob.

"Yada, yada, long story short, he called her sick and crazy, then left the dumbass with six figures of debt and divorce papers. Thankfully, she found a good friend who gave her a job and a place to stay while she finished college and paid off the debt. The end."

His gaze softened and he stroked hair away from her face. "Why haven't you told anyone?"

"I just told you, so you can leave now."

"I'm not leaving. Your ex-husband might have been a complete asshole, but that's not me." He tipped up her chin, making her look at him. "Give me a chance to be what you need, baby doll. What do you have to lose?"

There was a laundry list, starting with her self-respect. She'd lose someone who might have been a friend if she hadn't fallen apart in public so spectacularly, and probably her side hustle as a pro domme when everyone found out. He was right though. Things had to change.

Maybe she could give her little a few birthdays and let her grow up enough to stay home by herself. She could pretend to be a latch-key kid and... No, being a little didn't work that way—at least not for Lucia. She liked being six and a half.

She let out a trembling sigh and nodded. It might be okay if she thought of him as a babysitter instead of a daddy. Nothing would ever make up for losing Serena, but maybe he could keep her from destroying her life until she figured it out for herself.

All she had to do was not let herself get attached. Making love with him was right out. The feel of his hard chest under her hands made her want to let him do bad, bad things to her. She'd seen exactly what he could do to a woman and she wanted to cry, knowing she'd never have a chance to experience it for herself.

"That's my good girl," he crooned, stroking her back. "I'm proud of you for making a good choice." He hugged her tight, then kissed her temple. "You don't have to call me Daddy unless you're ready and you want to, okay?"

Every mature human had a child not ready to grow up, a logical brain that dealt with the minutiae of being an adult, and a mix of many other things. Enjoying Harry Potter as an adult didn't mean someone suffered from a personality disorder. Lucia was a proud Ravenclaw, thank you very much, and she'd be willing to bet Ryan was Hufflepuff, just like Serena had been.

Of course, Serena had never wanted to be sorted, so Lucia asked her the questions on the sly. She wondered if Ryan would do it.

Her little really wanted to call him Daddy, but her grownup was scared as fuck.

Her domme—the inner bitchy voice part—rolled her eyes at both of them. Hoping for the best, she crossed her fingers, then said, "Okay."

CHAPTER 3

*I*t took all of Ryan's fraying self-control to stop himself from demanding her fuckwit ex's name so he could go pound the loser into the dirt. It was no wonder she'd been so secretive about it.

He had to admit to some irritation with Serena too. Why hadn't she helped Lucia embrace her little instead of letting her hide?

"All right," he finally said, stroking her back. "Baby girls need their breakfast before they get surprises."

His arms didn't seem to want to release her, but he forced himself to let go. If he had any hope of helping her, he had to focus on her little. Then again, littles liked sitting in their daddies' laps. Daddies liked it too, but he had a big day planned for her. Taking her hand, he led her back into the kitchen.

"Where are we going?" She went to her seat and took a sip of coffee, looking at him expectantly. Her stuffed cat went on the table next to her.

He should have given her milk, but he'd used almost all of what she had for hot cocoa and pancakes. Then again, Ryan wanted to ease her into being comfortable showing her little to other people. Expecting her to automatically embrace what he was asking her to do wouldn't be productive.

Besides, judging by the selection of coffee in her pantry, he'd need to pick his battles. "It wouldn't be a surprise if I told you," he finally said.

"Will you at least tell me what to wear?"

"Jeans, comfortable shoes, and you'll need a jacket. We'll be outside most of the day. Wear something you don't mind getting dirty."

Frowning, she cut a bite of her pancakes, gathering a huge mound of whipped cream on her fork. "Do we need to stop by your place? All you have is your tuxedo."

"I keep an overnight bag in my car with a change of clothes. I'll get it while you're in the shower." Sitting across from her, he took a bite of eggs. "Will you introduce me to your friend now?"

She blinked and set her fork down, then cleared her throat and sipped her coffee. "Um… this is Princess Rainbow Kitty."

"Hello, your highness." Ryan bowed over the table, pretending to tip a hat. "Would you like some tea?"

A sweet, musical giggle burst forth, then Lucia blinked as if surprised it came from her. Point for the home team. Ryan hid a triumphant smirk and got an empty teacup from the cupboard, then set it in front of the stuffed cat.

"Thank you." Pink suffusing her cheeks, Lucia dropped her chin and finished her breakfast, plus a second cup of coffee.

"You're welcome." He nodded to the unicorn cup. "You're out of milk, but I saw orange juice. Would you prefer that?"

"No." She cradled her mug in both hands. "I might be little, but coffee is lifeblood."

"I agree." Standing, Ryan took their plates to the sink, rinsed them, then loaded the dishwasher.

"You cooked," she said, taking the skillet from him. "I'll clean up."

"Why don't you go tidy your room? I'll help you pick out something to wear once that's done." Although he wasn't surprised at her offer, he wasn't willing to let her back out of embracing her little today. She needed something else to do that would keep her in that mindset.

"Okay." She gave him a sweet, shy smile and grabbed her toy, then skipped up the stairs.

After finishing in the kitchen, he put on his pants and jacket, then jogged down the street to his car for his overnight bag. On the way back, he stopped at a bodega for a gallon of milk, then something in a shoe store window caught his eye. He'd polished Lucia's shoes often enough to know her size, and bought a pair of white sneakers with lights in the heels. Her little would love them.

Ryan let himself in and stopped for a moment, listening for noise. She was either still cleaning, or had already been in and out of the shower. Instead of interrupting her, he went downstairs to the play-room and used the bathroom there to clean up and dress.

The custom flooring, similar to cushioned rubber playground surface, looked a bit dusty, but would be fine with a good mopping. Although ferociously expensive, it was much easier to clean and disinfect than concrete, along with being a better surface for the tender knees of a submissive. Privately, he thought Serena cared more about Lucia's knees than anyone else's though.

White sheets covered all the custom bondage equipment, making it obvious Lucia hadn't been down there in a while. Smiling sadly, he lifted the sheet covering Serena's favorite spanking bench. Despite the months of disuse, it would be more than serviceable with a quick wipe down.

He and his best friend Mitch hadn't been the only ones spending whole afternoons with leather cleaner, beeswax furniture polish, and disinfectant. Serena hadn't given two shits that he and Mitch weren't really submissives. They cleaned too.

A good dominant is sensitive to what they ask of their submissives. How will you know how it feels if you don't experience it yourself?

Serena had said those words every time she had them do something unpleasant, and Ryan smiled wryly at the memory. It occurred to him to give Lucia a chore and have her clean up, but he didn't know if that would blur the line between little and grownup.

More than anything, Ryan wanted Lucia with him in the playroom. Serena might not be around anymore, but he remembered what it was like to have Lucia on her knees before him. This wasn't about him though. It was all about Lucia. She had to find her way back, embrace her little, and understand there were people who loved her no matter what. All of her—even her little.

After that, he had every intention of reminding grownup Lucia how much she loved to submit.

When he finished dressing, he went upstairs and grabbed a seat on the couch in the sitting room and scanned the news on his phone, growing more impatient. If they didn't get a move on, they'd miss her surprise. Grumbling softly, he grabbed the bag with her new sneakers and went upstairs. Soft humming emanated from her room.

"Lucia, are you…" Ryan blinked in surprise at the sight of her at her art table. She was covered in paint. Every toy in the room was piled on the floor, and the bed looked like she'd torn it apart. "What on earth are you doing?"

"Painting," she muttered, not looking up. "Princess Rainbow Kitty wanted a picture."

Do not let her see how angry you are.

"Okay." He cleared a spot on the bed and sat down, resting his elbows on his knees. "What are you painting?"

"It's a rainbow kitty like she is," she replied holding up a sheet of paper covered with what looked like every color she had. "What's in the bag?"

Reaching inside, he pulled out one of the shoes and tapped the heel, making the lights dance. She reached for it, squealing happily, but he returned it to the bag and out of reach. "Do you want to get paint all over your new shoes, baby girl?"

Her lower lip went out and she crossed her arms over her chest. "You're mean."

Interesting. She was acting out, purposely goading him into anger to see what he'd do. Judging by the challenging expression on her face, she expected him to either blow up or leave.

His irritation faded and he smiled. "These were a present for a good girl who was ready for her surprise. You're most definitely not ready for a surprise, are you?"

SERENA WOULD HAVE ROLLED her eyes and walked out, but aside from a momentary flare of anger in his hazel eyes, Ryan didn't yell or stalk away in a huff, or even give her the spanking she'd more than earned. Instead, he called her out. *And* bought her the light-up shoes she'd always wanted.

What was she supposed to do with that?

Lucia felt stupid. Ungrateful, childish, and flat-out dumb, and she hated seeing the irony there. He'd bent over backwards to help her get out of her funk of grief and sorrow. He had every right to leave, but he hadn't.

Lifting a hand to rub her face, she scowled at the swirled mess of paint covering her palms. "I'm sorry. That was incredibly rude."

"Stop." He didn't get up or raise his voice, and a small smile played across his lips. The scruff of beard shadowing his jaw looked so touchable and masculine. "Is your painting finished?"

"Yes, D… sir." Holy fuck, it almost came out, and she'd sworn she'd never call anyone daddy or mommy again.

Sir is one step below Daddy, baby doll.

Bitchy inner voices could just shut the hell up. Lucia could do sir. Ryan was most definitely a sir. He'd more than grown into an exceptional dominant since she'd met him. He took every lesson she and Serena ever taught him and added that *voice*. Lucia shivered, both with delight and trepidation, knowing he was up to something.

"Good girl. Now, do you still want your surprise?"

"Yes, sir." She dropped her chin, making hair fall in her face. Fuck's sake! Was that paint in her hair? What was wrong with her?

"All right." He got up and straightened the bed she'd made then torn apart. "Go get a shower and wash all the paint off. After that, we'll talk about what happened."

"I don't understand."

"You will. Go clean up."

She hurried to obey and shut herself in the bathroom, then scowled at the mirror. "Dummy, you could have skipped hair today, but you had to be a brat."

Jumping into the shower, she washed as quickly as she could, loading her wiry curls with conditioner so they didn't fuss. When she finished, she put on a robe and did a minimal makeup routine with tinted sunscreen and mascara. Her hair still wrapped in a towel, she returned to the bedroom, her knees shaking more than she wanted them to. Aside from the straightened bed, he hadn't touched the rest of the mess. She hadn't really expected him to though.

He carefully unwrapped the towel, then handed her a scarf and waited patiently while she got her hair safely contained.

"Much better," he said approvingly. "Sit next to me."

Although she tried, Lucia couldn't make sense of his expression. She was sure she was about to be punished, but he didn't look mad. Biting her lip, she sat on the edge of the bed, peering at him from under her lashes.

"Am I in trouble?"

"Maybe a bit." He traced a finger across her jaw. "But you knew that already, right?"

"Yes, sir." Lucia hunched her shoulders, but she... liked his soft voice, and his easy acceptance and patience. That didn't mean she wasn't going to have to pay the consequences. It just meant... Hell, she didn't know what it meant.

Serena... No, Lucia couldn't compare Ryan to her. They were different people, and it wasn't fair to either of them. She'd been Lucia's mommy, but...

With just a few words, Ryan made her feel more secure than she'd ever felt with Serena. She tried, and Lucia loved her for it, but being a mommy hadn't been Serena's favorite part of their friendship.

Ryan saw her. Really saw who she was.

"Good girl," he murmured, tucking the end of the scarf over her shoulder. "It's time for you to make some choices about what will happen."

"But what about my surprise?"

"Do you still want it? With a mess this big, I'm just not sure."

"Yes, sir, please."

He gave her a devilish smile, then patted his knee. "All right, here's your choice. You go over my lap for a spanking, then—"

There it was. Lucia knew she'd be punished eventually. She needed it, but the man had a deadly hard hand. "I don't want a spanking."

Without missing a beat, he said, "Let me finish. After I spank you, I'll help you clean up, and then we'll go to your surprise."

"What happens if I say no?"

"Then you clean up by yourself and we'll spend the day in the sitting room. No television, no toys, and no surprise."

Damn. Ryan might not have started out as a daddy dom, but he was pushing every one of Lucia's buttons. Sexy as hell, patient and gentle, and absolutely perfect. Before she knew what was happening, she nodded.

"Ask for it sweetheart," he murmured. "Tell me you want your spanking so we can move on to your surprise."

"I…" She swallowed hard, then peered up at him. "Please, spank me."

Leaning forward, he kissed her forehead. "I'm proud of you, baby girl. Go get the paddle I used last night, please."

Turning away before he saw her wince, she went downstairs. The hairbrush paddle was where they'd left it on the end table next to the couch. Her feet dragged, but she trudged up the stairs anyway. She had this coming, just as she had last night.

Although it was going to hurt, just knowing Ryan was there and cared enough to figure out how much she missed having a grownup taking care of her was more than she'd had in months. After hauling in a deep breath, she brushed away a few tears. No little wanted a spanking, but every one of them wanted to know they were loved even when they misbehaved.

"Good girl." Taking her hand, he pulled her close and kissed her cheek, then helped her drape herself over his lap.

The silk fabric of her robe bunched under her hips and she let out a gasp when he tugged it up over her bare ass. The sudden draft made her shiver, but she was comforted at the same time by the warmth of his thighs under her tummy.

"All right, Lucia. You know why you're getting a spanking, right?"

"Yes, D— sir. I painted and made a mess instead of getting dressed for my surprise."

"That's right," he said gently. "How many spanks should you get?"

"Five spanks?" This time, she'd make sure there was no confusion about what she was agreeing to.

He laughed and gently slapped her butt. "I was thinking ten."

"Seven spanks."

"Ten, but the first five will be with my hand."

Slumping, she pouted. "Ten spanks."

"Agreed." He leaned down and whispered, "Maybe it's a good thing you're little right now. I'm having a hard time stopping myself from taking you downstairs."

Oh. God.

Lucia's pussy clenched and a trickle of wetness dripped down her thigh, surprising the fuck out of her. She hadn't been interested in grownup play in...

She couldn't remember how long it had been. For the first time in ages, she wished she hadn't woken up little.

CHAPTER 4

*R*ound and firm, Lucia had the most amazing ass. Ryan resisted the urge to bite, and rubbed it firmly for several seconds as a warm up for what was to come. The paddle was sitting next to him, and she was ready.

Yet he held off. For some reason, he didn't want to spank her, even though she deserved it and had agreed. He'd never believed other doms when they said they didn't like punishing their subs, but it was true. Even Serena had told him that years before. Gritting his teeth, he waited for her to relax and brought his hand down smartly, making her generous flesh bounce.

"Ouch!"

She kicked her feet and wriggled, but settled quickly, thank goodness.

Whack!

Whack!

"Ow! D— sir, that hurts!"

Whack!

"A punishment is supposed to hurt, baby girl."

Whack!

Kicking again, she covered her ass with her hands. Catching both wrists, he held them still so he didn't hurt her, then hooked a calf around her legs to hold her in place.

"Are you going to make such a big mess before a surprise again?" he asked, reaching for the paddle with his free hand.

She twisted to look up at him, her gorgeous brown eyes glistening with tears. "No, I'm sorry. Can that be enough, please? I promise not to make a mess again."

"You're not in trouble for making a mess. You're in trouble for not obeying when I asked you to clean up and get ready for your surprise," he corrected gently. "Messes can be fun, but this wasn't the time."

Her face fell, but she nodded. "I'm really sorry," she whispered.

"I know, baby girl. But you're not going to get out

of your punishment. You have five more with the paddle. When we're done, you won't be in trouble anymore, and the misbehavior will be gone."

"Yes, sir."

She'd come so close to calling him Daddy more than once. He wanted to hear it, but didn't think she was quite ready. He'd have to wait and see how things played out.

Ryan rubbed the paddle in circles over her reddened bottom, giving her time to relax and get ready. When her head dropped, he brought the paddle down hard.

Thwack!

Thwack!

"Owwww, it hurts!"

She burst into tears, sobbing her heart out. Ryan wanted nothing more than to throw the paddle in the trash and cuddle her until she felt better, but he couldn't. She needed to know he'd keep his promises. As much as he hated it, he had to follow through.

"I know, baby." Redness blossomed on her golden skin, and he centered his next stroke on the lower curve of her ass, then quickly delivered the last two to the tender crease between her ass and thighs.

Tossing the paddle to the floor, he picked her up

and cuddled her in his lap, ignoring how far her robe had ridden up her legs. If he'd realized she hadn't been wearing panties, he'd have left it alone instead of tugging it over her hips. Holding her against his chest, he crooned nonsense words at her until she stopped crying.

She sniffed indelicately and took the handkerchief he offered. After wiping her nose and eyes, she tried to get up. Stretching, he grabbed Princess Rainbow Kitty. "Be still, sweetheart. We'll cuddle for a bit longer, then we'll get ready for your surprise."

Ryan pressed the toy into her arms, his heart aching when she buried her face in the plush faux fur. Finally, she looked up, adorable and so damned cute with little smears of mascara under her eyes.

"Thank you, sir. I feel better. Can we clean up now?"

"Sure." He helped her up and readjusted her robe so it fell to her ankles. "I'll get some rags and cleaner. You can put away some of your toys until I get back."

By the time he returned, most of the toys were put away and she was working on the bed. "Let's get the paint cleaned up and we'll leave the rest for later."

"Okay." She took the spray bottle of cleaner and a rag, then cleaned up the table while he picked up the wads of paper from the floor and dumped them in her wastebasket. Within a few minutes, the room was back to rights and no longer resembled the aftermath of Hurricane Little.

"This looks much better. Do you know what you want to wear?"

She chewed on her lip, then went to her closet. "Jeans and a sweatshirt, I guess. Will I get too dirty for my new shoes?"

"No, probably not." Ryan went to her closet and pulled out a pale pink long sleeved shirt with a sparkly unicorn on the front. There was a gorgeous ruffled party dress hanging behind it, but as much as he wanted to see her wear it, it wouldn't be appropriate for what he had planned. "Why don't you wear this pretty unicorn shirt? I bet you look beautiful in it."

With her golden skin, she probably looked amazing in whatever color she liked, and the pink would match the light pastel swirls in her scarf.

Shaking her head, she pulled out a dark blue sweatshirt. "I can't wear that in public."

"Why not?"

"Because it's got a huge unicorn on the front. It would be silly."

Ryan touched her chin, making her meet his

gaze. "Lucia, who cares? You'll look perfect for where we're going. Besides, it will match your shoes." Stepping back, he tapped his watch. "I'll wait outside while you get dressed. You have five minutes."

"What happens if—"

Two quick strides brought him to where he'd dropped the paddle. Crouching, he picked it up. "Do you really need to ask me that, baby girl? I want to see how pretty you look in your unicorn shirt."

Without waiting for her to answer, he walked out, shutting the door behind him. Although he'd seen her naked and in all manner of fetish wear on dozens of occasions, they weren't to that point in their relationship—if what they had could be called that. Right now, he was a glorified babysitter, yet he wanted it to be more. He might never have been anyone's daddy before, but finding out she was a little was it for him. It was something he'd never realized he wanted.

Hell, Ryan had been half in love with the woman since the day he met her. He never once acted upon it, of course. He'd always believed she and Serena were a couple, and he respected them both too much to go there.

Knowing there had been nothing between them

but deep friendship made it somehow better and worse at the same time. He didn't want to take away what Lucia had with Serena. He wanted... Hell. Just a chance. If he could just make her see...

Her bedroom door opened. Looking shy and a bit nervous, Lucia stood in the doorway, her new sneakers blinking. "Do I look okay?"

Lucia looked like a dirty old man's wet dream. She'd cleaned up the mascara and retied the scarf protecting her curls, letting a few strands loose around her face. The shirt fit her beautifully, molding itself to the contours of her generous breasts. Tight jeans covered her long legs.

"You always look gorgeous, but today you look like a sweet piece of cotton candy, and I want to gobble you up." Leaning toward her, Ryan pretended to chew on her neck, making her giggle.

"You can't eat me! I'm the gingerbread man!" Still laughing, she raced down the stairs.

Ryan followed, shaking his head.

LUCIA'S BUTT hurt and she was sore and tired from crying, but she never felt better. Well, at least not in a long time. Ryan was everything a daddy should be.

He didn't shy away from her little or tell her he didn't have time for games.

He didn't say she was sick in the head.

Even when he was in an obvious hurry, he'd been patient. He'd given her a choice of punishments, which was a novelty she'd never experienced or expected.

Ryan Sarver was everything Lucia had no business wanting.

It was so damned tempting to take what he offered, but how could she? She was a hot mess of whirling emotions, poor impulse control, and grief. Serena had been gone almost ten months. Why did it still hurt so much?

She couldn't even consider getting into a relationship. The time was irrelevant. Grief didn't have an expiration date, and grownup Lucia knew that. Her little wanted it to be over. She was ready to play and have fun again.

So, why hadn't Lucia let her? She didn't have to dress up and out herself at Saints and Sinners. She could adopt a pet, go to the park, or do any number of other things that would make her little happy.

They'd never been able to have pets. Serena loved cats, but was horribly allergic. Lucia could train it to walk on a leash and…

Ugh, be a crazy cat lady before she turned forty.

She wasn't home enough for a puppy though. It would have to be a kitty. Pets were therapeutic, right?

"Are you ready for your surprise?" Ryan asked, interrupting her thoughts.

Grabbing her purse and keys from the table in the foyer, she said, "Yes, please. I can't wait!"

"I'm glad, baby girl." He helped her with her coat, then led her outside.

It was a gorgeous day, crisp and sunny with big fluffy clouds chasing each other across an azure sky. A day like this made New York the best place in the world to be.

Kids were outside playing, people were walking dogs and pushing strollers. There was even an unattended hopscotch grid chalked on the sidewalk. Letting go of Ryan's hand, Lucia skipped it, balancing on one foot to pick up the small rock in one of the squares.

And nobody said a word about a grown woman playing hopscotch on a Brooklyn street corner. Ryan didn't either. He just waited on the other side of the grid and held out a hand for her with a grin on his face.

"Sorry, I know we're supposed to hurry."

"No worries." He tucked her hand around his arm and escorted her to his car, then opened the passenger door. "You were heading in the right direction, so it's all good."

Before she could reach for it, he drew the seatbelt across her chest. She inhaled the musky scent of his aftershave as he leaned over to fasten it. Lord, the man smelled good.

"Ready to go?" he asked, straightening.

"Yes, sir."

Nodding, he shut the door and strode around the front of the car to the driver's side, then got in. Easing his way into traffic, he soon left the surface streets for the freeway heading north. She frowned, wondering where they were going. Lucia didn't go into the Bronx much. In fact, it had been years since...

"Are you taking me to the zoo?"

He glanced at her out of the corner of his eye and flushed. "I should have blindfolded you. Yes, we're going to the zoo. After that, we'll have supper at this place I know in Little Italy." His attention on the road, he went silent for a moment, then added, "We can do the botanical garden or something else if you don't like the zoo."

"No, please! The zoo is perfect."

"Good." He pressed his foot down on the accelerator to pass some slower vehicles. "We'll just make our appointment."

"What? Who needs an appointment for the zoo?"

"That, my sweet baby girl, is a surprise, and I'm not saying a word until we get there."

Lucia pouted a tiny bit, but was too excited to see what he'd planned to risk bratting. "Just a teensy hint?" she wheedled.

"Nope. Now hush, or I'll spank you again before we go inside."

Although she thought she'd die of excitement, Lucia tried to stay patient and not ask any questions as he parked and hurried her in through the front gates. She even tried not to complain when he led her at a near jog past all her favorite exhibits. Eventually, they reached a building with a metal door marked with an 'employees only' sign.

Pulling out his phone, Ryan sent a quick text message, hiding it from her. A few moments later, the door opened, revealing a man slightly older than Ryan with thick dark hair graying at the temples and brown eyes. Tall and slim, his movements reminded Lucia of a very active bird.

"Hey, Ryan, I thought you weren't going to make

it." He held out a hand. "You must be Lucia. It's a pleasure to meet you."

"You too," she replied, shaking his hand.

"Sorry, we got caught in traffic," Ryan replied, ushering her inside. "Lucia, this is my friend Sam. We went to college together."

"Yeah, traffic. Anyway, let's get you covered up." He held out a set of gray coveralls, a mask, and a box of surgical gloves.

"What's this for?" she asked, putting on the coveralls before accepting gloves and the mask.

"We'll be going into a secure environment. I had to pull some strings to get you in because the—"

"It's a surprise, Sam. Let her see for herself," Ryan interrupted, slipping his mask over his face.

Sam flushed and gave her a sweet grin before pulling up his mask. "Oh, right. Almost forgot. Anyway, if you'll follow me, I'll take you to the surprise."

They followed Sam down a hallway painted industrial gray with tile floors, and Lucia squeezed Ryan's hand tight. She was excited, but scared at the same time. What could the surprise be?

Swiping a keycard to unlock it, Sam opened a metal door and led them inside. The room looked like a vet's office, with exam tables and other equipment she only vaguely recognized. She thought for a moment Ryan had set her up for medical play, but why on earth would he bring her all the way out to the zoo when Saints and Sinners had a very well-equipped room for that purpose? Aside from that, medical play wasn't her kink, which he well knew.

"Here we go," Sam finally said, opening a small cage. "This is… Well, we don't have a name for her yet."

Gently, he plucked something wrapped in a blanket from the cage, then turned and put it in Lucia's arms. She heard a squeak and pulled the edge of the blanket aside to reveal the whiskered face of a very young cheetah cub. Her eyes barely open, the baby peered up at her, then started to purr.

"Oh. My. God." She could barely breathe and her knees quivered. "She's so beautiful."

"Would you like to feed her?" Sam asked quietly.

"Can I?"

"I already have a bottle ready. Just have a seat in that rocker and I'll show you what to do."

Ryan helped her sit, and a few minutes later she was feeding a baby cheetah. Trying to hold back tears, she leaned over and kissed his temple even though their masks blocked actual contact. "This is the best surprise ever."

"Well, that's not your surprise," he replied. She heard the smile in his voice even though she couldn't see his lips.

"I don't understand."

"The real surprise is that you get to pick her name."

CHAPTER 5

It might have cost a fortune, but the look on Lucia's face was worth every penny. Her brown eyes gleamed with unshed tears and she looked up at Ryan with the most achingly sweet expression. He wished he could see the rest of her face, but no one could get close to such a vulnerable baby without being masked and gloved.

"So, what do you think? Do you know what you might want to call her?" he asked, snapping dozens of pictures with his phone.

"I…" She stroked the cub's rounded tummy, earning herself another purr. "Are you serious? I get to name her?"

"Yeah, your boyfriend paid—"

He drew a quick finger over his throat, cutting

off what Sam had been about to say, but Lucia was smarter than that and narrowed her eyes.

"I'm not going to ask how much you donated, Ryan, but you didn't have to do that. I'd have been happy with the goats in the petting zoo."

"You'll get to do that too," Ryan promised. "But now you get to name a cheetah, and she'll be your very own."

"I'm thinking she'll probably want to eat me when she grows up." Sighing, she closed her eyes, then pinned him with a stern glare that reminded him of her alter ego, Mistress Lucia. "No more surprises. I don't want you to spend money on me."

"Yes, ma'am," he murmured, brushing a piece of hair out of her eyes. "Have you picked a name for your baby?"

She cuddled the cheetah to her chest, humming softly as she rocked. "Her name is Nyota. It means star in Swahili."

"Good choice," Sam said, scribbling on the medical chart in his hands. "I like it."

Still cradling the cub, she stood, then handed her back to Sam. "We should probably let you get back to work."

Sam put the baby back in her cage, then shut the door. Looking at the floor, he stuffed his hands into the pockets of his coveralls. "No worries. I got some stuff done while you were feeding her."

She gave him a brilliant smile and threw her arms around his waist, hugging him tightly. "I know Ryan paid for it, but this was so amazing. I'll never forget it."

Blushing, he thrust out his hand awkwardly, nearly hitting Lucia in the face. "Anyway, Nyota is a good name, and I'm glad you liked your surprise."

He escorted them out, collecting the protective gear before wishing them a good day. Lucia smiled and closed her eyes, then turned her face toward the sun.

"Did you have fun?" Ryan asked, resisting the urge to pull her into his arms.

"That was amazing." She turned and stretched up to kiss his cheek. "Thank you."

"You're welcome." He led her away from the building. "What do you want to do now?"

"Can we see the primates? And then the petting zoo, and after that I want to see everything."

"Lead the way, baby girl." Smiling, he followed as she raced ahead, her new sneakers flashing in the sun. He loved watching her joy. It had been months since she'd last smiled.

She dragged Ryan all over the zoo, revisiting

several exhibits. He bought her an ice cream and his heart swelled at the sound of her exuberant giggles. He grabbed a napkin from the dispenser and wiped a smear of chocolate from her cheek.

"Daddy, can we…" The smile fell from her face and she turned away from a craft table where volunteers were laying out small pumpkins for the kids to paint. "Wow, that was awkward."

"Stop." He caught her hand and led her back to the art table. "Call me whatever you want, Lucia. You can call me Daddy, or sir, or Ryan if that's what works for you. All I want you to do is have fun today."

Biting her lip, she stopped walking. "Maybe we should just go. This is silly."

"Or maybe I should take you behind the restrooms and paddle your bottom until you get your head back in little space," he countered. "Don't let one small thing spoil your day, okay?"

"It's not exactly a small thing. I shouldn't have…" She shook her head and strode to the art table. "Just forget I ever said it, please. It won't happen again."

"Not hardly," he muttered, making sure she couldn't hear him. If she called him Daddy once, she could do it again.

He carried her pumpkin through the last few

exhibits she wanted to see. Although subdued and quiet, her face lit up with delight at the sight of a young woman with blonde pigtails and a bright blue smock doing face painting near the exit.

"Do you want a face painting?" he asked, making one last attempt to help her have fun. Although disappointed she hadn't enjoyed herself more, she probably hadn't been out as a little in a long time, if ever, judging by what he'd learned of her past. His baby girl would need baby steps.

"Can I?" She looked longingly at the artist, her face falling when the woman began packing up her paints. "Guess I was too slow."

"Come on." Ryan got a firm grip on Lucia's hand and dragged her to the painter. Smiling at her, he asked, "Do you have time for one more customer?"

"No problem," the woman replied, nodding. "Where's your little one?"

"Right here." He pressed down on Lucia's shoulders, making her sit on the stool across from the artist. "What would you like, baby girl?"

"I… I mean… I don't know." She tried to pull away, but he wasn't about to let go.

"How about a cheetah?" He pointed at the poster filled with sample designs.

"That's perfect. We just got a newborn cheetah in

the nursery." The artist didn't bat an eyelash and picked up a brush. "I think purple and blue. It will match your adorable unicorn shirt. Did your daddy pick it out? I love your shoes too."

Lucia blinked and her lips parted. "He's not my... I'm not a—"

"My daddy said I'd have to wait and maybe Santa would bring them." The artist continued speaking as if Lucia hadn't said a word. "Did you make your list for Santa yet? I want a big wooden dollhouse, and the giant teddy bear in the gift shop. My name is Melissa. What's yours?"

The artist kept talking as the drawing on Lucia's face took form. By the time she finished, Lucia was smiling once more, and chatted happily about trick or treating, sparkly shoes, and dolls. If those things made Lucia happy, Ryan was down with it. At least he had enough sense to keep notes on what she wanted to put in her Santa letter.

Holding up a mirror, the artist said, "You look so cute, see?"

Lucia turned toward the mirror and stared at herself for several seconds. A grin blossomed across her face, and she reached over to hug the artist. "I love it. Thank you."

"Yay! Give me your phone and I'll take a picture

of you and your daddy. Will you ask him if I can put my number in so we can have a play date?"

"Please do," he interrupted. "I bet Lucia would love to have a friend." Lucia did need a friend who was happily out with her little. Even better, he'd never seen Melissa at Saints and Sinners before. With luck, her daddy would be open to him picking his brain. Ryan didn't know much about littles beyond toys and teddy bear pancakes.

He had Melissa snap a picture with his phone as well, wanting a memory of Lucia looking happy for the first time in ages, then gave her a generous tip. By the time they finished, the sun was a thin sliver of red above the tree line. Zipping Lucia's jacket against the chill, he wrapped his arm around her and walked her back to his car.

Her lips parted into a shy smile and she looked up at him from the passenger seat. "I had a really great time today. Thank you."

"Me too." He buckled her seatbelt and gently brushed his lips over her temple. "Are you ready to be a grownup now?"

"Why are you asking?" She arched a brow and Ryan bit back a groan when her smile turned naughty.

To give himself time to formulate an answer, he

trotted around the hood and got in. He didn't want her to think he was expecting adult play because he wasn't. As much as he wanted that, he was after something bigger. Ryan wanted her to decide to put aside her little without being forced into it by him or by circumstance.

"Well, if you want to stay little, I'll take you for chicken nuggets. If you want to be a grownup, we'll go out for Italian."

"Candlelight, chianti, and cannoli?"

"Pietro's has the best puttanesca in town, and their caprese pizza is to die for."

"Sounds delicious." Her smile faded and she pulled the visor down, then grabbed a small pack of wipes from her purse. "I should probably clean this off."

Ryan caught her hand before she could touch her face. "Why?"

"Time to put away childish things," she murmured softly, grabbing a wipe with her free hand.

He tugged the wipe away and brought her fingers to his lips to kiss them. "Why, Lucia?"

Wasn't that the million-dollar question?

Lucia was a grown woman. She was in the Bronx, half an hour from her neighborhood, with a handsome man who was offering pasta and chianti.

"I don't want to be little," she said quietly. It was the truth, as far as it went. There was a part of her clamoring for those chicken nuggets, but she wanted to talk to Ryan as an adult and have a grownup meal. That meant washing off the pretty face paint. If she'd thought to bring a change of clothes, she'd have gotten rid of the shirt and light-up shoes too. She didn't want to though. Just the thought of wiping away Melissa's painting made her want to cry.

"Then don't be." He put his car into gear and drove from the parking lot, easily merging into traffic heading west into Little Italy. He put the wipe in a cup holder in the center console, appearing perfectly happy with the idea of taking her into a grownup restaurant looking like a kid.

Her patience fraying, she said, "Let me have the wipe, Ryan. I can't go to a restaurant with paint on my face."

"Hmm." He stopped at a light, then turned. "Let me ask you something. Do you have to put on a suit to be an architect?"

"Of course not. Well, not usually anyway."

"All right." The light changed and he turned his attention back to the darkened streets. "How about fetish wear? Does that make you dominant or submissive?"

"Where are you going with this? I… oh."

It might have taken her awhile, but Lucia finally got what he was asking. Sighing heavily, she looked out the window. "No, clothes don't determine who I am. I guess they're like a costume."

"So, if what you're wearing now is a costume, why do you think you have to take it off to share a meal with me?"

"Because I…" She paused, trying to formulate words for a concept she couldn't easily articulate. "Maybe my little is a secret."

"Is she?" He squeezed his car into a parking spot across from a small flower shop, then hurried around to help her out. "I mean, this is New York. You could walk around in a furry costume and nobody would bat an eye."

Looking down, she tried to hide a smile, but the sight of her light-up shoes made her laugh and shake her head. "True, but I doubt the other diners would appreciate it."

He pulled the tail of her scarf over her shoulder, then traced her jaw with a gentle fingertip. "You don't have to hide. Even if we weren't in New York, you're a beautiful, capable, intelligent woman, and nothing you wear will change that."

"But what will people—"

"Since when does Lucia Alvarez care what people think?"

"I was asking about you," she retorted. "Won't you be ashamed to be seen with me?"

Rearing back as if she'd struck him, he stared down at her. "Is that what you think?"

"I don't know." Lucia wished she'd never opened her mouth. Why did she have to spoil everything? "I'm sorry, I didn't mean it."

His jaw tightened and he pressed his lips together in a thin line, then moved into her space. His masculine aftershave washed over her in a heated cloud of delicious scent. "Are you a grownup now, Lucia?"

The low, throaty rumble of his words made her knees tremble and an immediate shot of arousal coursed through her veins. It wasn't his slow, deliberate Daddy voice, or the normal pleasant baritone of conversational speech. Lucia recognized a dom speaking when she heard it. It had been so long since anything had stirred her dormant sexual desire, she almost didn't recognize what she was feeling until he cupped her chin and tilted her head up.

"Answer me. Are you a grownup now?"

She probably should have been nervous, but she was too turned on. Swallowing hard, she tried to nod. "Yes, sir."

"Good girl." He stepped back and caught her hand. "We'll discuss this after supper. Until then, all you have to do is enjoy yourself and remember nothing you do will embarrass me."

Wrapping her hand around his arm, he escorted Lucia down the street, shortening his long strides so she could keep up. She wasn't one to submit on command. It was unfathomable how easily Ryan drew that part of her out. Although she'd dominated him in the past, it had been for his education. She gained no sexual pleasure from it, even though it had been enjoyable.

Being a domme was fun. She liked it, but it wasn't her thing like it had been for Serena. Dominance had been Serena's very identity, and Ryan was the same way. Even when he consented to submit to her or Serena, he wasn't a submissive. He did it to make himself a better, safer dominant. That was just the kind of man he was.

Lucia was a little and a submissive. That was her identity. Why shouldn't she be just as proud of those pieces of herself? They were part of what made her a whole person. Even though she knew many littles who were out and happy, she'd been too frightened of being judged by people like her ex-husband.

The truth was, she didn't know how Serena or anyone else would have reacted to her putting her little out there because she never tried. Serena hadn't forced the issue and had been perfectly content to let Lucia go her own way. The only times she'd ever acted like a mommy had been when Lucia specifically requested it, or did something naughty enough to make her respond.

Serena hadn't been into the dynamic, but had done it to make Lucia happy. That led to some rather painful self-reflection. Had she been playing at being a domme because it had pleased Serena?

God, she was a mess. Worse, Lucia felt guilty because she didn't know if they'd both done a *Gift of the Magi* thing, and given up a part of themselves to make the other happy. Thinking about how much better Ryan was at being a daddy made the shame that much more piercing.

Serena had been her everything for years, but they were best friends and their relationship had never been romantic or sexual, despite what they'd let everyone think. Had they kept each other from finding that one special person with whom they could have had a best friend and a lover?

It's in the past, baby doll, and life is too short to grieve forever. Time to move forward.

Although she couldn't get over how much it sounded like Serena, maybe Lucia's inner voice had a point. Serena wouldn't have wanted her to be unhappy, and would have definitely called Lucia out on her bullshit.

Letting go of Ryan, she ducked her head and pushed under his arm. He was so warm, and the scent of his aftershave swirled over her in a spicy cloud of masculinity and acceptance. How much trouble had he gone to for her zoo day? And all before she woke up, just so he could show her how it could be to let her little out.

He pulled Lucia into his embrace and walked her to a small storefront restaurant with a green striped awning, then opened the door. A gust of garlic and olive laden warmth made her mouth water.

With barely a dozen tables covered in ubiquitous red-checked tablecloths, the restaurant resembled any of a hundred family-owned bistros in the city. Recycled chianti bottles held candles, and small bud vases with multicolored roses were set on each table.

Most of the tables were full, meaning the food was probably good.

A server, her generous body wrapped in a white apron, rose from her perch on a barstool and approached them, then kissed both Ryan's cheeks, her eyes sparkling as a grin creased her lined face. "*Benvenuto*, Ryan! Looks like you two just came from the zoo. I bet you're hungry."

"Yes, very," Ryan said, helping Lucia with her jacket. "We'd like a table in a private corner if you have one."

"Do you mind waiting at the bar for a few minutes?" she asked. "I'll have one opening up shortly."

"Thanks, Mariana. Pietro's food is worth it." Cupping Lucia's elbow, Ryan led her to the bar and helped her up on a stool. "Can we get a few glasses of your house red, please?"

Grinning at Ryan's compliment, she filled two glasses, then left them alone. There hadn't been a word about Lucia's unicorn shirt, her shoes, or the face paint, and none of the other diners gave her a second look. Mariana didn't even ask for ID, and Lucia got carded almost every time she went out.

Had she been wrong all this time? Maybe it wouldn't be so bad. What would it cost her to let her little out? Her side hustle as a pro domme? Lucia hadn't taken a client since Serena's passing, so that wasn't an issue. She didn't need the money, and couldn't imagine herself doing it without Serena anyway.

Although she had no intention of finishing it, Lucia took a sip of wine, letting the sweet liquid give her a bit of courage. Even a little could be brave sometimes.

"Daddy?" She wasn't sure she intended the word to come out, but she wasn't sorry. It felt good to call Ryan that. Too bad she was scared as hell.

Without missing a beat, he lowered his head and kissed her temple. "What is it, baby girl?"

"Thank you."

He cupped her cheek, the feel of his callused palm sending prickles of need into her belly. Hazel eyes met hers and he brushed a soft, painfully sweet kiss over her lips. "You're welcome, sweetheart."

CHAPTER 6

*M*ariana led them to a quiet corner booth concealed from the rest of the dining room by a wooden screen painted with a map of the Italian peninsula. Although Ryan heard the low murmur of conversation, the noise wasn't intrusive. Private and secluded, it was perfect for his needs.

He'd had every intention of taking Lucia down into the basement playroom in her house and using whatever came to hand to explain what he thought of her. It irritated the fuck out of him that she still saw her little as an embarrassment.

But Lucia being Lucia, she'd turned things around and called him Daddy.

In the middle of a crowded restaurant, in front of

all manner of people, she called him the one thing he most wanted to hear and didn't try to take it back. He wanted to buy her that huge plush tiger from the zoo gift shop as a reward, but it would have already closed and she had more than enough stuffed animals.

Carrying her nearly full wineglass, she slid into the booth ahead of him. Instead of taking the other side, Ryan sat next to her, letting their thighs touch. Her familiar perfume slid around him in a cocoon of flowers. She smelled like summer and honeysuckle.

"You must have eaten here before," she said, flipping open her menu. "Everything looks amazing." Her hands shook slightly and she took another sip of wine.

"Yes. I have clients nearby and the lunch specials are very good." Gently taking her hand, Ryan stroked the soft skin of her inner wrist. "Let's share an antipasto tray. They do a good one with all sorts of hot and cold appetizers so you can have a little of everything."

Biting her lower lip, she nodded and let him take the menu away. "You can let go of my hand now. I'm not going to run away."

"I know." He kissed the tips of her fingers, tasting

her with his tongue. "Maybe I want to hold your hand."

Her cheeks darkened with a blush and she dropped her chin, yet her lips bowed up in a sweet smile. "I like holding your hand too," she whispered, her tongue darting out to lick her lower lip.

Ryan bit back a groan and tipped up her chin to meet his gaze. "I'm going to kiss you, Lucia."

Without waiting for an answer, he lowered his head and claimed her mouth. He should have given her time to consent, but when she buried her hand in his hair and tugged him closer, all thought fled and he lost himself in her taste and the feel of her. In all the times they'd been together, she'd never kissed him.

Letting out a soft whimper, she closed her eyes and deepened their kiss, then turned slightly, her thigh coming up to rest on his lap. Ryan thickened in his jeans, his cock surging almost painfully when she nipped him, then soothed it with a soft brush of her lips against his.

"Ahem."

Lucia squeaked and jerked away, her face flaming as they looked up at Mariana. Clearing his throat, he gave her what he hoped was a charming smile. "Sorry, we—"

Dark eyes twinkling with mischief, Mariana placed a tray filled with crusty bread and dipping sauces in front of them before refilling their wine glasses. "*Mi scusi*. I'm interrupting *una seduzione*."

"In Pietro's?" Ryan asked. "I would never."

"Don't fib to an old lady," she retorted, her happy expression belying her words as she snagged the menus. "Pietro is making the perfect supper for you and your *tesoro*. You'll need to keep up your strength to please her, yes?"

Apron flaring, Mariana bustled away. Sighing heavily, he rubbed his face and glanced at Lucia, giving her a shrug. She blinked once, then giggled.

"I feel like a teenager getting busted at the drive-in." She moved over, putting a few inches between them. "Too bad they aren't a thing anymore."

"We're not teenagers either," he muttered dryly. "Sorry."

"No, it's good." She picked up a piece of bread and dipped it in a dish of olive oil laden with herbs. "Open up," she ordered, grinning impishly. "You have to keep your strength up."

Ryan took the bread from her, swirling his tongue over her fingers to catch a few droplets of dipping sauce before they made a mess. Her pupils dilated and she gasped softly, then tried to pull her hand away.

Catching her wrist, he held her gently and cleaned the last of the herb-laden oil from her fingertips.

"Fuck, that's hot," she breathed.

Closing his teeth on the pad of her thumb, Ryan bit down, giving her a small nip. "Little girls shouldn't swear."

"I'm not little right now." She leaned close and licked the corner of his mouth, catching a stray drop of olive oil. "Big girls can say fuck."

"Big girls shouldn't say that word unless they're prepared to follow through," he countered, fully expecting her to back off and stop her teasing.

God, please let her back off.

"You're the one who planned this romantic dinner. Isn't that where we're headed with this?" She bit her lip and straightened, then looked away from him. "I thought... never mind."

"Tell me what you were thinking."

There had never been a time when he didn't want Lucia, but he wasn't about to take advantage of her when her head wasn't where it needed to be. Knowing she was a little along with being one of the smartest, most generous women he knew, was going to make it that much harder to resist her.

Ryan had a persistent fantasy of taking care of all

her needs. He wanted to be her daddy and her lover. Unfortunately, she wasn't ready for the demands he'd make on her as a grownup. She might never be, but he wanted to try.

"I thought this was a seduction." Her teeth worried at her lip again. "Maybe I was wrong. I'm sorry I presumed."

"You're not wrong." He tipped up her chin, tugging her lower lip from between her teeth. "I'd like very much to seduce you. I want to take you into the playroom and do all sorts of dirty things to you, but not until you're ready."

THANKFULLY, Mariana returned and rescued Lucia from having to answer Ryan. She wasn't sure what to say. How could they be friends when there was so much chemistry between them?

She'd never seen him as a love interest before, but the sparks of electricity arcing between them were unmistakable and powerful enough to make her wish she wasn't so broken inside. He was seeing her at her absolute worst, and she didn't want him to feel like she was his responsibility. How could he not see her that way after she'd been careless enough to let him learn about her little?

The one thing she knew with absolute certainty was that she didn't want to go into the playroom with him anymore. He was only saying what he thought she wanted to hear. Aside from that, nobody had been in the playroom in months, save the one time she went downstairs to cover all the furniture and empty the refrigerator of bottled water and aftercare snacks.

Well, nobody except Ryan. Part of her wanted to yell at him for invading her privacy, but there was no logical reason for him not to have showered in that bathroom. There was also nothing in the playroom he hadn't already used on multiple occasions.

It was one thing to race down the stairs for a paddle. Spending time in that basement with a man who wasn't into her was not on her list of things to do.

"Here we are!" Mariana said, a wide smile on her face. She either didn't notice the tension between them, or chose not to react to it. "To start, we have lobster crostini with champagne sauce." She put a small plate between them, then poured sparkling wine into a single flute. "A proper meal between lovers is shared."

Winking at them, she walked away.

It smelled wonderful, and Lucia almost forgot her irritation. She wasn't even really aggravated with Ryan. Her angst was directed mostly at herself. He had a point about picking up the pieces of her life. It was more than obvious she wasn't doing such a great job herself.

Mostly, she was tired of being sad. Maybe she wouldn't ever stop missing Serena, but that was okay. It didn't mean she couldn't find happiness without her. She just had to put forth the effort and let someone in.

She just wished it could be Ryan.

"My goodness, this looks delicious." She reached for a crostino, her mouth watering for the decadent treat.

"Ah, ah," he murmured, picking it up. "I'm supposed to feed you, remember?"

Holding a hand under the bite-sized piece of toasted bread, he put it to Lucia's lips. She bit into the appetizer and moaned in pleasure. Offset with creamy garlic spread, the astringent brightness of the champagne sauce woke up her taste buds for the succulent grilled lobster.

"That is so good."

"It must have been." He picked up a second and held it for her. "You're making sex noises."

"Am not."

His eyes crinkled with amusement. "Are too."

"Meanie." Trying to hide a smile, she took the food from him, nipping the tip of his finger before he could pull it away.

"Bad girls who bite might get punished," he warned.

Lucia's core clenched with a jolt of arousal. Knowing Ryan saw her as a pity date, she pushed it down. Instead of sinking back into her depressing thoughts, she decided to make the best of things. She picked up one of the remaining treats and held it for him.

"My turn to feed you."

He took it gently from her fingers, his eyes never leaving hers. She fed him the second one, her hand shaking. His stare was too intent and focused, and Lucia wasn't sure she liked it. He was probably waiting to see if she fell back into little space, but that was the last thing on her mind.

"Very good," he murmured, licking a drop of sauce from her hand. "I know why you made sex noises now."

"Ryan, I..." Biting her lip, she grabbed for her

water glass, then took a sip to give herself time to think. "Please, don't do that."

"Do what?"

"Don't make me think you… never mind."

Silent as a ghost, Mariana returned with the second course, a decadent bowl of sweet potato gnocchi with creamy herbed white wine sauce. She replaced the flute with a white wine glass and poured for them, then waited until Lucia took a sip. Sweet, yet crisp, it was probably the best wine she'd ever tasted.

"Oh, that's lovely." Lucia passed the glass to Ryan.

"Perfect. Thank you." He set the wine aside when Mariana left them alone again. "Finish what you were going to say," he ordered.

"I'd rather not." She picked up the fork, meaning to feed him a bite to shut him up, but he caught her hand, his long fingers covering hers.

"Tell me."

Huffing out a breath, Lucia jerked away. "Don't pretend you want me, Ryan. I get that I'm a project for you, but please don't lead me on."

His eyes hardened and he crowded her against the wall, his big body towering over her. She held his angry stare, unwilling to back down, but couldn't help a small squeak of surprise when he grabbed her hand and put it over the very hard bulge in his jeans.

"Do not," he gritted out, "think for one single second I don't want you."

"But—"

"Be quiet. You are one word, one sip of wine, and one bite of gnocchi away from being dragged from this restaurant and bent over the hood of my car because I want to fuck you so hard you forget your own damned name."

"I—"

He grabbed the tail of her scarf, pulling her head back, then touched gentle lips to the sensitive spot under her ear and kissed her, sending shards of electric desire down her spine. "And I'll make sure you always remember mine."

Heat blossomed in her core, filling Lucia with sudden need. She couldn't let him fixate on her though. She was a train wreck waiting to happen. "Ryan, I get it. You have the white knight thing going on, but this isn't going to work. I'm too messed up."

"You're not messed up, baby." He pulled her against his warmth and reached for the fork, then fed her gnocchi dripping with sauce. "You're sad and scared right now, and that's okay. I'm going to try my best to make you happy again, but nothing is going to happen between us until you ask for it."

Lucia rolled her eyes. "Look, you're a great guy, and I appreciate what you're trying to do, but I'm not going to change my mind. I'm definitely not asking for anything to happen between us."

"Hmm." He held the glass to her lips, allowing her to take a sip. "We'll just see about that."

CHAPTER 7

$\mathcal{M}$ ariana returned with the next course, making Lucia slam her lips closed on what Ryan was sure would have been a snarky reply. When he arched a brow at her, she tilted her nose in the air and looked away.

He might have to spank her for bratting later.

For now, they were going to indulge in Osso Bucco with wild boar and creamy polenta. Pietro had outdone himself with this dish, but Ryan was too busy watching Lucia suck the tender meat from the bones to taste it. The way her tongue wrapped around the...

He shook his head in a desperate attempt to get the image of her doing the same thing to his cock out of his brain. One night together wouldn't convince her how good things could be between them. Instead, he needed to show her they could be more than temporary play partners.

The thought made him pause. As much as he cared for Lucia, he wasn't sure he was ready for a relationship with anyone. Yet the thought of letting her go, or worse—seeing her with someone else— made him seethe.

"Cat got your tongue?" she asked, swiping a piece of bread through the leftover sauce from the boar. She held the bite for him with a napkin underneath to catch drips.

"No, I..." Ryan ate the bread from her fingers, trying to think of something to say that wouldn't scare her off. All he needed was a little time so he could figure out if this was really what he wanted. More importantly, he had to know if Lucia would consider him as more than a friend who happened to bully his way into her life.

Hell, who was he kidding? All she had to do was say the word and he'd do almost anything to make her happy—even if it meant letting her go.

Boy, you have it bad. You need to tell our baby doll how you feel.

What the hell? Where had that come from? He frowned, shaking away the random thought.

A slightly dishonest idea came to mind. "I was just thinking I have to take off early tomorrow morning. I completely forgot my landlord is renovating my kitchen next week. I have to clean out the cupboards and arrange for a hotel room."

It wasn't even a lie. Although Ryan wasn't required to leave, he'd already arranged for a hotel room so he could work without the renovation noise. He was counting on Lucia's altruism. She'd opened her home to guests needing temporary lodging many times.

"You can stay in the guest room," she replied. "It has its own bathroom so we won't be in each other's way. You can use Serena's... I mean the office if you need to work."

"Are you sure? I don't want to put you out."

"No." She frowned and bit her lip. "It's fine. I mean, it won't be for more than a week or two, right?"

"That's what my landlord told me." Ryan crossed his fingers in his lap, hoping something would come up to delay the construction crew.

"Okay. I'll help you with your kitchen in the morning." She folded her napkin and laid it on the table. "I am so full," she groaned, crossing her hands over her stomach.

"Not too full for panna cotta with fresh raspberries, I hope," Mariana said, setting a small plate on the table along with two coffee cups. "It's my daughter's specialty."

"It looks delicious," Lucia said, smiling at Mariana. "Thank you."

They reached for the dessert at the same time, but Ryan got there first. He scooped up a small bite and held it to her lips, biting back a groan when she licked the creamy custard from the spoon. Laughing softly, she took it from him, then fed him a bite.

"Maybe I should have Mariana pack us a serving to go," he murmured, taking the spoon from her.

"Oh?" She accepted another spoonful, letting out a small whimper of pleasure.

A drop of raspberry sauce clung to her bottom lip. Leaning close, he swiped it away with his tongue, then kissed her. The gentle brush of her lips across his sent a spark of electricity down his spine.

"I was thinking of very naughty things to do with that dessert."

She gasped softly, then shook her head. "Stop teasing me."

Ryan kept his voice calm and even, but he wanted to shake her for not believing him. He had no idea what to say to make her understand he wanted grownup Lucia just as badly as he wanted her little. "Who said I was teasing?"

"You…" She leaned away from me, refusing the next bite of custard. "Look, I'm a little. I like playing with toys and wearing shoes with lights, and—"

"Does being a little mean your grownup self doesn't have needs?" Ryan asked, interrupting her. "Do you have to be one or the other?"

"No." She frowned and rubbed her forehead. "I don't know. Maybe? Doesn't the thought of having sex with a little weird you out?"

"You said yourself you're not always little," he countered. "You're not little right now."

"Way to evade the question."

"I don't want to make love to you when you're little. I want to cuddle you and take care of you."

"But what if—"

"Lucia, enough." Ryan cupped her chin, forcing her to look at him. "I loved taking care of your little today. I had an amazing time at the zoo with you. I also like when you dominate a sub almost as much as I like watching you submit to a dominant. All those parts are who you are inside. I won't make you choose between them, and I'm not going to stop wanting you."

Her eyes flickered with interest. "Does that mean you'll submit to me again?"

Chuckling softly, he shook his head. "Don't press your luck, baby girl. You know I've never been submissive."

"What if I have something new to teach you?"

"Then we'll talk. But I seem to recall you and Serena both said I learned everything I needed to know." Leaning close, he whispered, "Are you telling me you were holding out on me? I might have to spank you for that."

LUCIA SHIVERED, her core spasming with desire at the sound of Ryan's husky voice. He made a very good point too. Hadn't she just told herself to trust him?

Knowing he'd be willing to submit to her again to learn a new skill made her wish she had something else to teach him. Hell, who was she kidding? Him admitting he'd be willing to discuss it had her about melting into a puddle of wet need.

This would be completely different from their past scenes. It would be just the two of them, and she wouldn't be his teacher. She'd be his submissive for real this time, and she wanted it so, so badly.

But she didn't want to be a pity fuck.

"Are you…" She swallowed the last of her coffee to give herself time to think. "Are you serious, Ryan? It's okay if you don't—"

He leaned close and nipped the shell of her ear. "Did I not demonstrate how serious I was earlier when I put your hand on my cock? I'm still hard for you, and there will be consequences the next time you doubt my word."

"I…" Lucia cleared her throat, trying to get something intelligent to come out of her mouth. "I don't know what to say to that."

Tipping up her chin, he touched his lips to hers in a gentle kiss. "All you have to say is yes or no. You know how consent works, and nothing will happen between us without it."

She rested her forehead on his shoulder. "It's been a long time since my last date. This sounds stupid, but I don't want to be a pity scene, you know?"

Ryan huffed out a breath and tugged her into his arms. "You are definitely not a pity date, Lucia. Get that thought out of your mind right now because

I've been about half in love with you since the day we met."

"But… you never said a word."

"Honey, I thought you were with Serena," he reminded her. "I wasn't about to come between you."

"It wasn't like that," Lucia said softly. "We were best friends, and not just because she helped me after my ex-husband dumped me. I loved her, but we never… I guess you could say we weren't *together* together."

"She was your beard," Ryan replied. "You used her to hide your little, but I don't want you to do that anymore."

"I was hers too." Lucia laid her head on his chest, listening to the reassuring sound of his heartbeat. "Our pretend marriage kept our clients from expecting more from us, and we were open enough in our relationship that we both had our needs met."

"Clever of both of you." He laughed softly, then finished his coffee. "Let me ask you something. When did you learn about your little? Has she always been there?"

"I'm not sure," she replied, deciding to be honest. "My ex liked naughty schoolgirl roleplay and it kind of fit since he was about ten years older than me. We both enjoyed it, but at some point I realized I loved the part that built up to our scenes."

"How so?"

"Well…" She bit her lip and tried to formulate a coherent thought. "We had a spare room set up as a classroom, so I got a desk and a whiteboard from a school auction. It didn't seem right, so I bought paints and kid's books, then some stuffed animals." She glanced sideways at him and smiled. "Anyway, you get the idea. It was comfortable for me, and it gave me a chance to forget about my real classes and pretend I didn't have to adult for a few hours."

"Would you have stopped being a little if you knew he didn't like it?"

"I'd have never started," she whispered, tears pricking her eyes.

"That would have been a crime." He took her hand and kissed her fingertips. "If you knew you'd have my support and protection, would you let your little be seen?"

"I could ask you the same question." She straightened to meet his gaze. "I'm terrified, Ryan. I'm scared to death people will judge me, but I'm also scared they'll judge you."

"First off, you know perfectly well the littles at Saints and Sinners don't get treated like that.

Besides, I'm a big boy and I can't think of anything I'd enjoy more than being your daddy."

"But—"

He laid a finger over her lips. "Hush and let me finish. I don't care if people judge me, because they're not important. You are all that matters to me."

Lucia nearly melted into a puddle of goo. How the hell did Ryan always know the exact right thing to say? "I..." She let out a breath, trying to control her racing heart. "Okay, Daddy. I'll try."

His tight hug nearly stole her breath. "I'm proud of you, baby girl. Thank you for being brave for me." Letting her go, he stood and held out a hand for her.

"I'm not," she replied, sliding out of the booth after him. "I'm still scared shitless."

"It's okay." He laid several bills on the table, then escorted her outside. "You just need to understand that I'm going to be there for you whether you're little, or domme, or sub."

"I don't have a problem with the last two," she muttered, matching her steps with his until they reached his car.

He helped her in, then buckled the seatbelt around her hips. "You don't have a problem with your little either," he countered. "You just need a daddy who isn't an asshole."

Without waiting for her to respond, he shut the door and walked around to the driver's side and got in. She choked back a giggle, then said, "That's what Serena called him too."

Funny, instead of making her cry, the memory of Serena chewing on her ex-husband after the divorce hearing made her happy. It was a wistful sort of poignant joy, but she felt better.

"Maybe you should call him that too." Ryan waited for a break in traffic and eased his car from his parking spot. "Let's hear you say it."

"I thought I wasn't supposed to say bad words."

Giving her an encouraging smile, he waved a hand for her to continue. "It's a special occasion. Go on."

She let out a breath, then said, "Frank Marshall is an asshole."

Lucia had blamed herself for too long, and it felt good to finally put into words what she should have said years ago.

"Louder and put some feeling into it," he replied, merging onto the expressway taking them south toward Brooklyn.

"Frank Marshall is a pencil-dicked asshole with a neck measurement bigger than his IQ!"

Ryan jerked the wheel and tires screeched as he jerked to a stop on the shoulder. Wrapping a hand around her neck, he pulled her into a thorough kiss, devouring her like he was starving. Nipping her lip, he tangled his tongue with hers until she whimpered and tried to crawl into his lap.

Traffic whizzed by, horns blaring. The blast of an air horn passing too close finally pulled them apart, and they stared at each other for several seconds while the car rocked in the wake of the truck's slipstream.

Laughing softly, he rested his forehead against hers, then stroked her swollen lower lip. "That's my good baby girl."

CHAPTER 8

*R*yan let out a sigh of relief, thanking his lucky stars he hadn't killed them both. Darting across two lanes of a busy interstate just to kiss her hadn't been one of his better ideas.

"Are you okay?" he asked, straightening her seatbelt.

"I'm…" She put her hand over her mouth and closed her eyes.

"Lucia, honey, answer me, please. Are you hurt?"

She shook her head, her hand still over her mouth. Without warning, she snorted, then burst out laughing. Rolling his eyes, he waited for a break in the oncoming cars and got back on the expressway.

"I'm sorry." She glanced at him, then giggled. "That was terrifying, but it was really funny."

"You are very naughty," he said, chiding her gently. In truth, he wasn't the slightest bit angry. It was too good to see her smiling.

"I'm not the one doing illegal lane changes. If I was still in the domme business, I'd have taken a crop to your ass."

"True, but I am sorry I scared you."

"It's okay." Reaching for his hand, she squeezed his fingers and held on for the rest of the drive back to her brownstone.

He didn't even mind when she nodded off, and smiled at her cute little snores. Parking down the street from her house, he nudged her awake. The face painting was smeared around the edges from her nap, but still recognizable.

"Hey, baby girl, we're home."

She jerked awake and sat up, blinking owlishly. "Wow, sorry. I didn't mean to conk out on you."

"You're fine. You had an exciting day." He got out, then went around to her side of the car and held her door. It wasn't necessary, but he liked the old-fashioned courtesy, and especially liked her accepting it.

When she shivered, he pulled her close, enjoying the feel of her pressed against him as they walked.

"Hey, you said something in the car that made me curious."

"What was that?" She pulled her keys out and unlocked the door, then hung her purse and coat on the tree.

He followed suit, slipping off his shoes when she did. "You mentioned something about not being in the domme business anymore. Were you serious?"

"Yeah, kinda." Lucia went into the kitchen and pulled a filtering water pitcher from the refrigerator, then poured them each a glass. "It was always Serena's jam, you know? I was just along for the ride."

"You were good at it."

She sat down at the kitchen table, her hands wrapped around her glass. "Thanks. It's not that I didn't enjoy it, and maybe I'll do it again someday, but without her…" She took a sip of water, then let out a heavy sigh. "It's just not the same."

"So, you'll be a sub the next time you go to Saints and Sinners?"

"Probably." She finished her drink and put the glass in the dishwasher. "Would it bother you if I went as a little?"

He blinked, then finished his water to hide his surprise. "No, but as scared as you've been to let your little out in public, I'm concerned it would be too fast."

Giving him a crooked smile, she nodded. "You're probably right, but maybe I can go to one of the monthly play dates."

"That's a wonderful idea. The Halloween party for the littles is tomorrow, in fact." Leaning over, he kissed her cheek. "Be patient with yourself, Lucia. It doesn't all have to happen in one day."

She bit her lip and looked away. "I know. I just… I really like you, and I don't want you to get tired of my bullshit."

Somehow, he managed to resist the urge to pump his fist in triumph. "That's not going to happen," he said firmly, taking her hand to lead her from the kitchen. "We'll talk about it tomorrow, but it's time for baby girls to go to bed."

"I… okay." Walking toward the stairs, she added, "I'll help you change the sheets on the guest bed first."

"I can do it. Just show me where the linens are."

"No, I need to clear out some of my stuff anyway. That's my room when I'm not being little."

Now that he knew there hadn't been a romantic relationship between her and Serena, he understood why she had her own room, and kept her little space separate from where she spent time as an adult. He followed her up the stairs, then helped her retrieve clean sheets from the linen closet. "I can use the couch so you don't have to give up your room."

"I'm not going to make you sleep on the couch for a week. That would be rude when I have the space." Glancing across the hall, she sighed sadly. "Actually, maybe it's time I did something with Serena's room. I haven't been in there since she died."

"Do you want help?" he asked gently, wrapping his arms around her from behind.

"I'd like to be able to say no, but I'm probably not that brave," she confessed. "I just—"

"It's okay. I'll help you when you're ready."

She turned in his arms and reached up to cup his cheeks. Tugging him down, she kissed him, her tongue tracing along the seam of his lips. Groaning, he swept her into his arms and pressed her against the wall. He needed to stop before things went too far, but he couldn't by himself. Having Lucia in his arms was everything he'd ever wanted.

"Baby girl," he whispered, tracing his lips over the sensitive skin under her ear. Her sweet floral scent nearly made him forget what he wanted to say. "We can't."

"Why?" She nipped his throat, soothing the sting with another kiss.

"Because—"

"Are you waiting for a planned scene in the playroom? We don't need it."

Lucia was right. They didn't need anything, and he'd wanted her for years. Pulling away, he held her still and stared into her fathomless brown eyes. "Are you sure, honey?"

Flushing, she looked away and bit her lip, then tried to wriggle free. "Awkward. Sorry."

"No, you don't." Dropping the fresh sheets, he slung her over his shoulder and stomped into the bedroom, then slammed the door behind him.

"What are you doing?" She wriggled again, making him swat her butt.

"I asked you if you were sure," he replied setting her on her feet. "Because if you say yes, I'm not letting you go."

LUCIA SWALLOWED HARD, the feral set of his jaw making her knees shake. She wasn't afraid of Ryan. He'd never hurt her. Well, not unless she asked for it. She was afraid of what he promised.

A future with someone who accepted her. A lover, daddy, and a friend all wrapped up in one incredibly sexy package. And all she had to do was take that first step and take what he was offering.

But what if he didn't mean it?

What if he does? Take a chance, baby doll.

"Do you…" She took a breath and looked up. "Are you serious?"

"Sub, domme, and little, I mean it." He tugged her scarf loose, letting her curls spring free in a wild halo around her face. "You'd better be sure about what you're asking, because if you say yes, I'm not letting you go without a fight."

"Please, don't let me go."

"Never," he whispered, sinking his hands into her hair.

Lucia melted against him, tears pricking her eyes. This was everything she'd ever wanted, and all she had to do was accept it. "Make love to me?"

"I have condoms in my bag." He tightened his grip on her hair, then kissed her hard enough to steal her breath. "Give me ten seconds."

Without waiting for her answer, he was gone and she heard his pounding footsteps on the stairs. Rolling her eyes, she opened the nightstand drawer and pulled out an unopened box. A few seconds later, he burst back into the room, waving several wrapped condoms.

"I think you forgot where you were," she murmured, holding up the box she'd retrieved. "There are condoms scattered all over the house."

He blinked at her and smiled wryly. "Good point." He dropped the protection on the bed and stalked her, tugging his shirt off to reveal washboard abs with a scattering of dark hair narrowing to a delicious treasure trail. "Undress for me, sweetheart."

Instead of obeying, she crossed the room and put her hands on his chest, loving the feel of hard muscle and hot man under her fingers. Even his rich, masculine scent revved her motor like nobody's business. "I've never touched you before," she murmured, leaning against him. Crisp hair rasped against her cheek, sending a delicious tingle into her core.

"I beg to differ." Ryan stroked hair away from her face, letting the curls twine around his fingers. "Don't tell me you don't remember pegging me."

Lucia giggled and lifted her face from his chest to smile at him. She didn't usually like people playing with her hair, but it felt wonderful when Ryan did it. "Yes, but I've never touched you like this before."

"Like what?"

"Like a lover," she whispered. "Like I'm touching the man who's going to make love to me."

He chuckled softly and traced a finger across her jaw, then down the center of her chest. "I am definitely that. Now, are you going to undress as I asked, or am I going to spank you?"

She caught the hem of her shirt and lifted it, baring a few inches of her abdomen. "Can it be both?"

"It can be whatever you want," he replied, helping her ease the shirt up and over her head.

"I like the sound of that." She fumbled at the front clasp of her bra, letting out a soft moan when he brushed his fingers across the lace covering her sensitive nipples.

The cups fell away, revealing her to his avid gaze. "I like the sight of that," he murmured, bending to take a turgid bud into his mouth.

"Oh, God." Lucia's head fell back and she grabbed his hair, pushing him against her breast. He groaned and circled her nipple with his tongue, then nipped. The sting sent a bolt of electricity into her core, making her hiss out a breath of delight.

"You taste like candy," he murmured, reaching up to give her neglected nipple some attention. He traced his finger over the stiffened nub and her belly quivered. "Have you ever come from someone playing with your nipples?"

"N-no." She'd seen other people do it, but had never experienced it for herself. Maybe Ryan would be the one to…

"Oh, fuck!"

Slowly, inexorably, he pinched her nipple, making it throb. He released the pressure, then squeezed again like a sentient nipple clamp that knew exactly when she was about to cry uncle.

"Maybe we'll experiment. I think I'll try wax." He tightened his fingers, then loosened them oh so slowly. "I'll let the candle drip on your pretty nipples to get them all sensitive for me, then use a Wartenburg wheel, or maybe a vampire glove. What do you think about that?"

Breath catching, Lucia nodded dumbly. She hadn't submitted to anyone in such a long time, and it was almost as if she was a brand-new sub who had never experienced D/s play. It didn't seem to matter that she'd taught him most of those skills herself.

Hell, as long as it had been since her last sexual encounter of any kind, she might as well have been a virgin again. Thankfully, she remembered to make her appointment with the aesthetician before the

Halloween Masquerade. Although Ryan had seen her lady bits already, she was glad to have taken the extra step, never knowing anyone would actually be seeing her naked.

He had the perfect soft, slightly growly baritone that made her insides quiver and her core dampen with need. It was a voice one obeyed without question, and it didn't seem to matter that they weren't actually sharing a scene.

"Use your words, Lucia," he prodded gently. "I need to hear you consent."

She swallowed the massive lump in her throat, then said, "You know I do. I wouldn't have let you touch me otherwise."

"Nope. I want you to tell me all the naughty, dirty things you want me to do to you." He grinned crookedly, then added, "Make it very detailed and show me how to make consent sexy."

Oh, mercy. The student is schooling the master.

She unbuttoned her jeans and slid them off to give herself time to think of something to say, but left her pink silk thong where it was. "I want you to play with my breasts."

"And?" He unzipped his jeans, then moved to the bed and stretched out, lounging against the headboard. Pulling his cock free, he stroked himself as he watched her intently.

"Um…" Her throat went dry and she fixed her eyes on his hand clenched around his shaft. It didn't even matter that she probably still had paint on her face.

"What am I going to do after I play with those gorgeous breasts?"

"I want to taste you."

"Good choice. I want to taste you too. Tell me what you'll do to my cock, baby girl." He curled his hand around the crown, spreading precum down his shaft.

"I want to suck you," she whispered. "I want to play with your balls when I take you into my mouth. I want to play with your ass. I wish I had more hands so I could do everything at once. And I want to swallow everything when you come."

"Very nice," he whispered, holding out a hand glistening with moisture. "Come here and taste me."

It never occurred to her to disobey. Kneeling on the bed next to him, she took his fingers into her mouth and licked them clean of the salty sweet deliciousness. His warm hazel eyes were fixed on her face and he watched her with unconcealed desire.

"You taste good."

"I bet you taste better," Ryan countered, tugging her hand until she laid down on her side facing him. "Tell me what else you want."

I want everything.

She swallowed the words before they came out, then licked her lips. "Maybe it's time for you to show me how sexy consent can be. Tell me what you want."

CHAPTER 9

I want everything.

Ryan held the words inside, knowing Lucia wasn't ready to hear them.

Pushing her gently to her back, he got to his knees and loomed over her. "I want to feast on you like a fucking Christmas dinner."

"And?" Her left eye closed in a slow wink. "Show me how consent can be sexy."

"Hmm." He eased himself between her thighs and inhaled the perfume of her heated arousal through the scrap of panties. "I want to lick your pretty pussy until you come. Do you consent?"

"I could be convinced to allow it." She arched her back and pushed a hand into his hair, tugging gently. "What else do you want?"

"I want…" He lowered his head to her belly just above her mons and pressed a soft kiss against her skin.

Ryan had to be gentle with his baby girl. He couldn't tell Lucia what he really wanted.

Her on her knees. Obedient and willing. Beautifully submissive and open. Trusting he'd meet all her needs. He wanted to keep her safe and happy. She'd have everything she ever desired for as long as she allowed him to stay in her life.

"Ryan? Are you okay?" She slipped free and sat up, then cupped his face in gentle hands. Her worried expression nearly undid him. As damaged and grieving as she was, her first thought was for him.

"I'm good." He blinked wetness from his eyes and kissed her palms, then said, "Lie back, baby girl."

"Are we done making consent sexy?" A slow grin twitched her lips upward."

"Not quite." He pulled himself together before he spilled all the things he wanted to say. "Tell me you want me to fuck you until you speak in tongues."

Rolling over, she pushed him to his back and straddled him, her damp sex sliding against his cock. She leaned down and nipped his ear, then licked away the sharp sting.

"I, Lucia Alvarez, want you, Ryan Sarver, to fuck me unconscious. I want it rough. I want dirty and hard, and I want to have bruises in the morning." Lowering her head, she kissed him, stealing his breath until he couldn't speak. "How's that for consent?"

He dug desperate fingers into her ribs and rolled over until she was on her back. "I want to take you into the playroom," he hissed, pushing his painfully hard shaft into her belly. "I want to lay you over the spanking bench and tie you until you can't move, and then I want to flog you. I want to push a piece of ginger in your ass and make you suck my dick until the burn makes you scream."

"Whoa." She pushed him away and got up, then sauntered to the door.

Fuck. He'd gone too far. Ryan's head fell back to the pillows and he rubbed his face. "Lucia, I'm sorry."

She turned, her gaze speculative as she laid a hand on her hip. "Last one downstairs is a rotten egg. Do you consent, baby dom?"

Getting to his feet, he stalked toward her, "I'm not a baby dom anymore. You saw to that."

"Prove it." She disappeared around the corner.

Chuckling wryly, he tucked himself back into his jeans and zipped up before following her down the stairs. She always did have a tendency to top from the bottom. Then again, she was used to teaching newbie doms. She probably didn't get the opportunity to submit to someone who knew what they were doing very often.

From the kitchen, he heard the sound of the refrigerator opening and closing. She appeared a moment later, carrying bottled water, a bag of cubed cheese, and a bowl filled with grapes. It was simple and easy food for aftercare. Considering the state of the playroom, he doubted there was anything in the downstairs refrigerator worth eating.

"Let me help," he said, taking the food from her.

"Thanks." She chewed on her lip, then peered up at him. "Are you sure—"

"Go downstairs," he ordered. "Put the water in the fridge, then take the sheet off the spanking bench and wipe it down." She blinked and opened her mouth, but he cut her off with a raised finger. "After you finish, you will sweep the floor around the bench, then select the implement of your choice from the rack of impact toys and clean it."

"You can't just—"

"Stop." He laid a finger over her lips, unsurprised when she tried to nip him. "Are you currently emotionally and intellectually able to give consent?" He pulled his hand away, allowing her to answer.

"I already did, but I'm still worried you don't want me."

"Yes or no, baby girl," he interrupted. "My consent is not in question. I've already told you how much I want you, and not just for one night."

"Yes, sir."

"Good girl." Softening his tone, he laid his hands on her shoulders and kissed her forehead. "I want your head in the game, Lucia. I want you to focus on me and not on feeling inadequate or broken, or whatever other words are running through your head that flat out aren't true. I'm not going to let you top from the bottom this time either. You're going to get five spanks for every time you've questioned me because that's not how a submissive treats their dominant, and you know it."

Cheeks turning pink, she nodded and looked down at her feet, a shy smile blossoming. "I'm sorry, sir."

"Good girl," he murmured, pushing a wayward strand of hair behind her ear. "You have five minutes, and when I come downstairs, I want you kneeling next to the bench. Tell me what the correct position is for a sub about to be punished."

"Sitting on my heels with my knees spread and my eyes down, and holding the implement out for you," she whispered, cheeks still flushed.

"Well done." He took a step back, then added, "Are you going to top from the bottom?"

"No, sir." She grimaced and looked away. "I'll try not to anyway."

"That's all I can ask." He turned her to face the stairs, then swatted her butt. "Five minutes, sweetheart."

She squeaked and went to the top of the stairs, her feet stalling on the edge as she looked down.

C'mon, baby girl. You can do it.

He crossed his fingers, trying to be patient, then let out a sigh of relief and set a timer on his watch when she went down the stairs.

This had to be hard for her. She wasn't the only one harboring secret second thoughts though. Ryan wasn't sure this was the right course of action for her. Would it do more harm than good?

Unfortunately, he couldn't think of anything else to do that would pull her out of her funk. She had to realize he loved her no matter what.

His knees shook and he stumbled to the couch before he fell. He... loved her, and always had. He couldn't tell her yet though. How could he when he could barely say the words to himself?

A good dominant experiences things before they ask their sub to do it. Be as brave as she is and tell her what's in your heart.

Jerking his head up, he blinked. He would bet money Serena had whispered those words, but that wasn't possible. Snorting, he went to the kitchen and drank a glass of water.

Months after her passing, Serena's presence still filled the house. It was no wonder he was hearing things.

AFTER PUTTING the water in the fridge, Lucia grabbed a broom from the utility closet where the cleaning supplies were kept, along with rags and disinfectant. It was almost comforting to have a chore to keep her mind off her whirling thoughts.

Instead of focusing on the spanking bench like he asked, she stripped the dust coverings off all the furniture, and replaced the linens on the king-sized bondage bed just in case things went well and they ended up sleeping in it.

Ryan was perfect, and she didn't understand why

he'd want to be with her when she was such a mess. He was right about her letting her thoughts get away from her though. All she had to do was believe what he told her. Ryan didn't lie. If he said he wanted to be with her, then he did. It was almost a relief to give him her trust.

Wasn't that the way things were supposed to be between a dom and a sub? There was freedom in giving over control to a trusted partner, and she desperately wanted someone to help her carry the weight of her sorrow. Even if she and Ryan didn't work out, it could happen with someone else in time.

That was a sticky point though. Lucia really wanted it to be Ryan.

Tell him what you want, baby doll. You know better than to assume what people are thinking.

For once, her inner voice was right. It just meant she'd have to screw up some courage and do it. She shook herself and got back to work wiping down the spanking bench. Her time had to be running short, but at least the sweeping was already done.

"You have one minute left, baby girl," Ryan called from the top of the stairs.

She raced to the implement rack and chose a crop at random, wiped it down, then put away the cleaning supplies. Steadying her breathing, Lucia knelt in position next to the bench, held the crop on outstretched palms and lowered her eyes to a spot on the floor between her knees.

Ryan's feet were almost silent on the stairs, and she settled her mind, waiting patiently for his next order. The simple act of lowering herself to her knees cleared her thoughts and she closed her eyes at the sensation of overwhelming peace. How had she gone without this for so long?

"There's my good baby girl," he murmured, putting the aftercare snacks in the refrigerator. "You did a beautiful job."

He still wore jeans, although he'd zipped them. It didn't seem possible, but he was sexier now than he'd been when he was playing with his cock. His abs bunched and rippled, making her want to lick a path down his treasure trail.

"Thank you, sir." She shivered with pleasure at the approval in his voice and dropped her hands to her splayed knees when he took the crop. Peering up through her lashes, she tried to look at him without being caught.

"You're welcome." Taking her hand, he helped her to her feet and turned her to face the spanking bench. "Tell me why you're going to be punished, please."

"Because I... I didn't trust you when you said you wanted me."

"That's right. You're going to get five for every time you doubted my word. Twice in the restaurant, and once just before I sent you downstairs. How many is that?"

Lucia hauled in a breath and nodded. "Fifteen, sir."

"Thank you. Do you have a personal safeword, or do you want to use stoplight colors?"

She used to have a personal safeword, although she hadn't needed it in years. Maybe it was weird, but she didn't want to use the one she'd had with her ex-husband. She didn't give a shit what Frank thought, but it seemed almost disrespectful to use it with Ryan.

Maybe someday, she and Ryan could choose a new one.

"The stoplight, sir." This wasn't the right time to call him Daddy, but with every sir, she relaxed a little more. Maybe this could work. Just as she had a separate room for her little, Ryan could have a separate name for his dominant.

"All right." Laying a hand between her shoulder

blades, he pushed her down until she bent at the waist and her chest met the thickly padded leather of the bench. "I'm going to trust you to be still while I punish you, Lucia. Use your safewords if you need to, understand?"

Tugging gently, he pulled her panties down to her ankles, then lifted each foot in turn to get rid of them.

"Yes, sir." There was no way she was going to safeword over a cropping, but it was nice that he offered. Hell, a punishment might finally drive home the knowledge that Ryan cared and wanted what was best for her.

As thick as your head is, I'm surprised he's not beating you like a drum, baby doll.

She closed her eyes and sighed, relaxing into the welcome embrace of a submissive mind space. Her inner voice, which still sounded too much like Serena for her comfort, could wander off and bother someone else.

"Are you ready to get started?" he asked, stroking her back. His touch felt so damned good.

"Yes, sir. I'm ready."

"Good girl. I want you to count them."

Without giving her time to prepare herself, he brought the crop down, the stinging blow nearly making her lift up on her toes. Blowing out a breath between pursed lips, she said, "One."

Thwack!

"Two."

Thwack!

"Three."

She counted the next several, wishing she'd chosen an implement with more thud and less sting. "Ouch!"

"Count or I'll start over," Ryan warned.

"Eight, sir." She couldn't keep her heels on the floor any longer and tears streamed from her eyes.

Thwack!

"Nine." It was whispered through tears, but she managed to keep counting.

He stopped and petted her bottom, soothing the pain from her cropping. Wiping her wet face on her arm, she risked a peek over her shoulder. "Sir?"

Toying with the crop, he said, "The last six are going to be hard, Lucia, but these are important. I want you to count the next three, but I also want you to listen to me very carefully."

"Yes, sir. I'll listen to you."

"Good girl."

Thwack!

She bit back a cry. "Ten."

"I'm glad I'm your daddy because I enjoy watching you play and have fun."

What?

Thwack!

"Eleven." Tears fell in earnest and she had to concentrate on his words.

"I'm glad I'm your daddy because I can't wait to take you trick-or-treating, and see what Santa brings you for Christmas."

Thwack!

"Twelve!"

"I'm glad I'm your daddy because I get to take care of you." Leaning closer, he pushed her hair out of her face and kissed her. "Being your daddy is everything I never knew I wanted, and being your dominant is a dream come true."

Using the crop handle, he tipped up her chin to make her look at him. "For the rest, you're going to tell me three things you like about being my baby girl and my submissive. Can you do that?"

"I…" Her thoughts spun. Ryan was everything she ever wanted in a daddy, but what could she say without scaring him away? "Yes, sir. I think so."

CHAPTER 10

This might be a punishment, but it was also positive reinforcement. He hoped the cropping would help the lesson stick. If not, he'd do it again and again until she believed it. But the most important part hadn't happened yet. She needed to vocalize those good feelings and internalize them.

Ryan gave her a moment to gather her thoughts, then brought the crop down on her upper thighs, making her screech.

"Thirteen!" she cried.

"Tell me a positive thing, sweetheart," he prodded gently.

"I'm glad you're my daddy because..." She hauled in a breath and started over. "I'm glad you're my daddy because you gave Princess Rainbow Kitty tea with breakfast and didn't laugh at me."

Thwack!

"Fourteen." She sniffed and wiped her face on her arm. "I'm glad you're my daddy because you give the best cuddles, and because you don't get mad even when I'm being naughty."

"There you go, baby," he crooned. "Just one more and we'll be done, but I'm so glad to hear you tell me those things."

As much as it stroked his ego to hear what she was thinking, this wasn't for his benefit. She needed to listen to herself say those things. He stroked the red welts on her bottom, deciding to place the last one on the crease between her thighs and buttocks. It was the one spot he'd avoided because it hurt like fuck.

Thwack!

She cried out the number and dropped her head to the padded leather, sobbing her heart out.

Dropping to his knees, he cupped her cheeks and kissed her tears away. "There's my brave girl. I'm so proud of you. Tell me one more thing and we'll be done."

In a whisper so soft he had to lean close to hear,

she said, "I'm glad you're my dominant because I've fallen in love with you."

Without warning, she wrenched herself free and scrambled off the bench, then raced for the stairs. He chased after her, catching her in his arms before she got to the second step.

"Did you mean it?" he demanded, caging her against the wall when she tried to wriggle away.

"I…" She caught her breath and looked down, her misery palpable. "I'm sorry. You don't have to say it back."

"I'll ask you one more time." He cupped her jaw, making her look at him. "Did you mean it, Lucia?"

She let out a breath and nodded. "Yes, sir. I love—"

He didn't wait to hear the rest and kissed her hard, burying both hands in her hair to hold her still. Whimpering, she dug her short nails into his shoulders, the sweet sting going straight to his balls. She gave as good as she got, sucking his tongue into her mouth, then letting it go to nip at him.

"Say it again," he husked. "Tell me you love me one more time, baby girl."

"I…I love you, Ryan." She looked away, her cheeks reddening. "But you don't have to—"

"I've been in love with you almost since the day I

met you." Letting go of her hair, he picked her up, groaning when she wrapped her legs around his waist. Backing away from the wall, he put a hand under her ass to keep her in place and strode to the bed. He sat and scooted over until he leaned against the headboard, then settled her in his lap. "I never thought I'd get to say it, much less hear you say it first."

"You really meant it," she breathed, resting her head on his shoulder. "I didn't believe you in the restaurant."

"I trust it won't take another cropping for you to realize I mean what I say."

Sniffing inelegantly, she shook her head, then said, "No, sir."

Grabbing a tissue from the box on the table next to the bed, he wiped her tears away, along with the last of her cheetah face painting, then held it to her nose. "Blow, sweetheart."

She obeyed and he finished cleaning her up. "That's better," he murmured, tossing the tissue in the wastebasket. "If you're ready to continue, I need a color."

Giving him a smile, she nuzzled her face into his chest. "I'm green, sir. And…" She sat up and rested her forehead against his.

"What is it, honey?"

"I wanted to say thank you. I think I needed a come to Jesus moment to make me realize I'm not going to be sad forever, and…well, it was really nice to let my little out with you today. I didn't know it could be like that."

"Are you sad now?"

Pursing her lips, she thought for a moment, then shook her head. "I'm not. I still miss Serena, but it…" She crawled off his lap and sat next to him. "You know what's strange?"

"What's that?"

"Sometimes, I think I hear her." Lucia laughed softly and leaned against him. "I know it sounds crazy, but you know that inner voice everyone has that tells them when they're doing something dumb?" When he nodded, she said, "Mine sounds like her."

He hesitated for a split second, then said, "It doesn't sound crazy at all. I think maybe I've heard her too." More than once, in fact. A shiver coursed down his spine and he decided not to share that tidbit with Lucia. It was creepy as fuck, but comforting at the same time. It was almost as if Serena was still looking out for them.

Throwing back her head, Lucia laughed until she snorted. "She's haunting us."

"Hmm." He turned to face her and gave her a wicked smirk. "She was always a voyeur. I bet she's waiting for a show. Do you want to stay here, or go back upstairs?"

"Upstairs." She glanced around and grimaced. "The place needs some work, doesn't it?"

"It's nothing a few subs and a little elbow grease won't cure." Ryan helped her to her feet, then up the stairs.

"I seem to recall you did an excellent job on the wood fixtures," she replied, closing the door behind them. "And my shoes haven't been the same since you graduated from our little bondage academy."

"Ah, but I'm not the sub anymore."

Grinning, she winked. "Well, if the polishing cloth fits, sir."

"You're asking for another spanking, baby girl," he warned, trying to hold back a smile. He had every intention of helping with the chore, but he was too delighted she'd regained her sense of humor and quick wit to say anything.

"I already had my spanking. Isn't it time for you to fuck me and leave bruises?" she asked, backing slowly toward the stairs. "You said yourself we need to give Serena her show so she stops haunting us."

Grinning, he stalked her slowly, wanting to give her a chance at the very naughty game he was quickly putting together. "If you can make it up the stairs before I catch you, you'll get a treat."

"What happens if you catch me?" she asked, laying a hand on the banister.

"Then I'll get a treat." He took another step toward her and cracked his knuckles. "Run, baby girl."

LUCIA RACED UP THE STAIRS, trying to stop giggling. Ryan was so freaking funny when he tried to look threatening. She knew better though. He was a big teddy bear at heart.

Her butt still hurt, but it had been ages since she'd actually had fun while submitting to someone. Working with a baby dom just wasn't the same as having a partner who knew what he was doing and truly focused on her.

Without warning, he caught her just as her foot touched the top step and swung her over his shoulder. She let out a noise that was somewhere between a panicked scream and a laugh when he carried her into the grownup bedroom and slammed the door.

He put her down, letting her slide down the front of his muscular body, but didn't let go. "All right. Serena's gotten her show, and I've got my gorgeous submissive right where I want her."

Leaning toward him, she licked his nipple, then bit gently. "What are you getting for your treat?"

"My favorite thing," he said huskily, dropping to his knees. He caught her hips and pulled her close, then buried his face between her legs and sucked her clit into his mouth.

"Oh, fuck." Her knees wobbled and she rested her hands on his head to keep her balance.

Letting out a soft growl of appreciation, he let go of her hip with one hand and pushed a finger inside her, then curled it to massage her g-spot, never letting up the suction on the tender nub at the apex of her sex.

Her backside pulsed, still aching from his cropping, but it only added to the overwhelming pleasure coursing through her body. "I never taught you that," she said, gasping for air as her core clenched and spasmed, heralding the mother of all climaxes.

Without warning, he pulled away, leaving her hovering on the edge, the bastard. She bit her lip against a sob of disappointment, knowing he wouldn't relent quite yet.

"I'm a gifted amateur." His face glistening with her arousal, he stood and led her to the bed.

"Hardly." She followed, her knees still quivering. "You were holding out on me."

His lips twitching into a wry smile, he unzipped his jeans and let them fall to the floor, revealing his naked body in all its glory. "All you needed to do was say yes, honey."

"I'm saying yes now." She stepped into his embrace, wrapping her arms around his waist. "Make love to me, Ryan. Please."

"With pleasure." Lowering his head, he took her lips in a deep, deliciously gentle kiss that made her toes curl. "Tell me you love me again."

"I love you again," she whispered, kissing her way across his jaw and down his throat.

"Smart ass." His lips met hers again, searing her soul. "Get a condom, baby girl. I want you to put it on me and make me wish I was already making love to you."

He laid on his back, propping his shoulders on several pillows, then stroked his cock. The sight of him playing with himself made Lucia's mouth water.

"I did teach you that," Lucia murmured, tearing

the wrapper open. She wanted to hear him say he loved her back, but wasn't about to beg for it. Instead, she knelt on the bed next to him and licked the crown of his dick, making him hiss out a breath.

Turnabout was fair play. Lucia took him into her mouth, relishing the salty sweet of his precum as she sucked him. Licking her way down his turgid shaft, she cupped his balls and massaged his perineum with a gentle finger. She wanted to edge him just as hard as he'd done to her.

Ryan bucked his hips, thrusting into her mouth. "Honey... Oh, God."

Knowing he was too close to climax, Lucia backed off and lifted her head, then eased the latex down his shaft. "Give me a color, baby boy."

"This is definitely topping from the bottom," he gritted out between clenched teeth, corded tendons straining in his neck. He lifted his hands, then dropped them back to the bed.

"Are you complaining?"

"Yes." Sitting up, he lunged for her and positioned her straddling his hips. "I'm also green, so why don't you fuck me until you leave bruises."

"Hmm." She stretched out over him, then brushed kisses over his chest. "Is that supposed to be an offer I can't refuse?"

Sobering, he cupped her cheeks. "We can both refuse at any time, Lucia. You know that."

"I know." Leaning down, she pressed her lips against his, then traced the edge of his teeth with her tongue. "But I hope you don't."

"Same, baby girl." He stroked gentle hands down her back and cupped her ass, his fingers digging in.

It almost hurt, yet having his hands on her felt too good. She slid her pussy against him, loving the tease, but both of them were too desperate. Reaching between their bodies, she closed her eyes and positioned him at her entrance, then lowered herself, taking him deep inside.

"Oh, fuck." It had been so long, and felt so damned good. He filled her completely, making her clench and spasm around him.

"Move, baby," Ryan murmured, thrusting up into her. "Show me how you like it."

Arching her back, Lucia laid her hands on his chest and flexed her hips, the slight pinch of pain from too long without sex fading. Ryan kept his gaze fixed on her, his hazel eyes warm and filled with need. Stilling, she leaned down to kiss him, their tongues dueling for control. He wrapped his arms around her and stroked her back, holding her like she was the most precious thing in his world.

The feel of him cradling her in his warm embrace while he loved her was indescribably good, making her blink back a tear of overwhelming joy.

Letting out a groan, Ryan rolled her to her back and caught her thigh, holding her open as he surged into her harder and faster.

"Tell me to stop," he said, his voice a low rumble that sent a fresh wave of intoxicating pleasure into her. "I wanted this to be slow and gentle, but—"

"Don't stop, please!" The change in position sparked new sensation to life and she bucked against him, crying out her pleasure.

Taking her hand, he pushed it between their bodies. "Touch yourself, baby, but don't come until I tell you."

Lucia touched her slick flesh and the scant brush of her fingertips over her clit nearly made her explode. Keening softly, she eased her hand away. She was too close to the edge to obey.

He slid out, leaving her empty and wanting. "Ah, ah," he chided softly, nipping her ear. "Keep going."

"I can't." She whined softly, gritting her teeth as she tried to obey. The climax gathering force in her belly rushed into a swirling conflagration, making her pant with need.

"Just a little longer, baby." Lowering his head, he

took her nipple into his mouth, his sucking kisses sending a fresh spark of electric passion coursing down her spine.

"Oh, God." She touched her clit again, feeling the hot slide of him against her fingers. Her hips bucked uncontrollably as he fucked her. Lucia clutched at his shoulder with her free hand, her nails digging deep into muscle in a desperate attempt to hold it together just a little longer.

He stopped moving and cupped her chin, holding her gaze. "Tell me you love me, Lucia."

It was so not the right time to confess love for someone. He had to know that, but she wanted to hear him say it too. "I…"

Damned needy doms. Say it, then make him say it back. You know you want to.

"I love you, Daddy."

Shuddering, Ryan fisted her hair and thrust inside her. "I love you back, baby. So, so much."

It was everything she needed, and he didn't even wait for her to ask. "Please," she whispered. "I can't—"

He thrust into her, seeming to touch the core of her soul. "Come for me, Lucia."

"Oh, fuck!"

As if it was waiting for his permission, the climax

she'd been trying to hold at bay surged free and she exploded into a thousand pieces of quivering, sated bliss. Aftershocks rocked her and her core spasmed around him, making him hiss out a breath.

Kissing her softly, he quieted her whimpers and slowed his movements, rocking into her with languid thrusts. "There's my good girl," he whispered, sliding his hand between their bodies to pinch her clit. "Give me one more."

"I..." The sudden pressure sparked her arousal all over again and she let out a breathless scream when he increased the pace of his thrusts. Bucking under him, she tried to meet his body with her own as a second orgasm swelled in her belly, almost painful in its intensity.

"I'm going to make love to you like this at least once a day," he gritted out, nipping the side of her neck under her ear. "I love watching you come apart under me."

"Yes!" She clutched his shoulders, hanging on for dear life. His muscles clenched, bunching under her hands, and she inhaled the thick scent of masculinity and spice, the fragrance of their sex making her head spin.

He let go of her clit and eased his hand under her ass, lifting her hips. The new position changed the angle of his thrusts, letting his cock drag across her g-spot.

Brushing his lips across her mouth, he kissed her so gently and sweetly, it brought tears to her eyes.

"Come for me, sweetheart."

Although she wanted to hold it back just a little longer, Lucia was too overwhelmed and sensitive to do anything but obey. Her orgasm lacked the hard edges of the first, welling in a gentle tide of sensation that swept her away on a rising current of bliss so profound she lost the ability to speak or breathe. Blinded to everything but him, she gave in.

CHAPTER 11

*I*f it were physically possible, Ryan would have made love to Lucia forever. Watching her come apart under him was the most beautiful thing he'd ever seen, and he'd never tire of it.

Unfortunately, he wasn't going to last, and counted himself lucky he'd managed to hold on long enough to give her that second climax. His orgasm built at the base of his spine and he shuddered. Balls aching, he kissed her hard, deepening the connection between them.

"God, Ryan." Lucia sank her hands in his hair, pulling him closer.

"I know, baby." He breathed the words against her lips, then surged inside her one last time. His eyes crossing at the overwhelming pleasure of making love to his woman, he spilled inside her.

His heart thundered in his chest and he collapsed to the side, then drew her into his arms, pulling her tight against his chest. Her perfume mingled with the scent of their sex into a heady cloud and he inhaled deeply.

"Mmm." She reached behind her and fumbled for the box of tissues, finally dragging one free. Easing back, she took care of the condom and dropped it into the wastebasket.

"We should clean up," he murmured.

She burrowed her face in his chest and sighed, then wrapped a leg around his hip. "No, I'm comfy here. This is your life now."

Ryan chuckled and kissed the top of her head, then got up and covered her with a sheet. "I'll get a washcloth and a towel."

A soft mumble came from under the sheet and she waved a hand. Smiling, he hurried across the hall for a warm cloth and a towel, then returned. When he touched her, she didn't respond.

"Poor baby girl." Trying not to wake her, he cleaned her up as best he could, and dropped the used cloths in the bathroom hamper. Retrieving his phone from his jeans pocket, he set it on the nightstand, then spooned himself around her curvaceous body.

He wondered if she'd wake up tomorrow as an adult or a little. Either one would be just fine with him. As he was about to drift off, his phone chimed with the tone he'd set for Ebony. Biting back a growl, he went into the hall and answered.

"Hey, Ryan. There's been a power surge at Richards and Richards," she said, yawning in his ear. "I tried to troubleshoot over the phone, but I think the main server is toast. Caroline wants someone there ASAP. I also ordered a replacement, which should be here tomorrow morning. I paid extra to get it before nine."

"Thanks." He tried not to grimace at the shipping expense. It couldn't be helped, and certainly wasn't Ebony's fault. "I appreciate you trying, and for getting things started on the replacement."

"No problem. Do you want me to meet you?"

"I'm good. It's after midnight, and I'll want you at the office tomorrow to receive the delivery. It would be a huge help if you'd drive it over too."

"Sure thing. Sorry to disturb you so late."

"These things happen, and it's definitely not your fault. I'll see you tomorrow."

Ending the call, he grabbed his clothes and

dressed in the bathroom. He couldn't stand leaving Lucia alone, but he also couldn't ignore his business. He tiptoed into the bedroom Lucia used when she was little and scribbled a note on a piece of art paper with a purple marker, making a half-decent effort at drawing a kitten on the bottom.

As an afterthought, he mentioned the Saints and Sinners Halloween party. If memory served, the club supplied costumes for the littles. There would also be trick or treating. Lucia would love that, and he'd hopefully be done with the server in time to meet her there.

Just in case she didn't have it, he added his phone number as well, asking her to text him when she woke up.

He left the note on the nightstand, then brushed his lips over her temple and gave her Princess Rainbow Kitty to snuggle.

Although he'd miss out on sleeping with Lucia, there would be other nights, and other opportunities to cuddle with his baby girl. If he was very lucky, the problem would be easily fixed and he'd be back in her bed before she knew he was gone. At the very least, he ought to be home in time to cook her breakfast.

He drove across town and parked in the underground lot. The whole office building was dark, meaning he had a long night ahead of him. Cursing, he walked inside, meeting the owner and a security guard in the lobby.

It might have been rude, but he didn't stop to chitchat. At the very least, he needed to secure the backups before the battery power supplies failed. Dim security lighting lit the corridors, but the only illumination in the office was a pair of flashlights.

"Have you found out when the power will be back on?" he asked the owner, Caroline Richards.

"Not yet," she answered. "They wouldn't give me an estimate."

"Okay. Give me about an hour to finish these backups. I have another server coming in the morning, but I won't be able to do anything until the power comes back on. I'll do what I can, then come back then."

"That isn't acceptable."

He rubbed his temples, not bothering to hide his irritation. "There is no power, Ms. Richards. What do you expect me to do?"

Ryan resisted the urge to ask her if she wanted him to rig up an exercise bike to a generator. Knowing how demanding she was, he'd bet she'd jump on the idea.

"I'm paying you a lot of money to keep these computers running," she snapped. "The least you can do is stay in case the power comes back. I also have a contract, so you have to agree to reasonable requests."

Thankfully, his contract with Caroline would be up in December. Although it was going to cost him a fortune in lost revenue, he wouldn't be renewing it. Even though he'd be billing her for every minute of time he spent with his thumb up his ass, there was only so much he was willing to tolerate from a client and she'd stepped over the line. It might be more professional to tell her, but he was only required to give her thirty days. That was exactly what she was going to get.

"Fair enough," he finally said. "I assume you'll be staying as well."

"Of course not. It's one in the morning." She walked out, closing the door behind her.

"Thank God for small favors," he muttered, redirecting the flashlight. It took all of fifteen minutes to secure the backups. Still irritated, he settled into the receptionist's surprisingly comfortable chair and tried to get some sleep.

LUCIA BLINKED, squinting at the bright sunlight blazing in from her bedroom window, then realized she held Princess Rainbow Kitty instead of Ryan.

Phooey.

Maybe he was downstairs making breakfast. She wouldn't mind having teddy bear pancakes again, but a smoked salmon omelet from the kosher deli on the next block over sounded pretty wonderful too. Besides, she'd eaten an entire week's worth of carbs the night before. She sat up and rubbed her eyes, then glanced at the clock, shocked at the time. She never slept past eight, and it was already almost ten.

"What's this?" She reached for the sheet of art paper on the nightstand and read Ryan's note, both disappointed he was gone and thrilled he'd let her know where he went. Taking the note with her, she ran downstairs to get her phone and dialed his number.

"Ryan Sarver speaking," he snapped.

Lucia blinked at his sharp tone. "Hi, um... it's Lucia. Is this a bad time?"

"You have perfect timing." His voice softened. "Good morning, baby girl. I'm sorry I'm not there to make you breakfast."

"It's okay. You had to work." Thinking quickly,

she added, "I was thinking about going to the deli for an omelet. I can bring you something if you want."

"No, but thank you. I had some bagels and coffee delivered a few hours ago. Did you just wake up?"

"Yes, Daddy. I slept really well. Will you be back soon?" She almost said home, but managed to hold the word back just in time. He might have said he loved her, but that was a long way from moving in.

"Good girl." He let out a sigh and she heard the sound of his fingers tapping a computer keyboard. "I'm going to be at least another three or four hours, so I want you to go to Saints and Sinners for the Halloween party, okay?"

"But…" Her lower lip went out and she shook herself. Now was not the time to drop into little space and act like a spoiled brat. He'd obviously been up all night, when she'd been sleeping like the dead.

"What is it, baby? Do you need me to come home?"

Lucia's knees almost buckled and she dropped into a chair before she fell. She loved hearing him say that, even if she hadn't had the nerve to do it herself, and just knowing he'd abandon his job for her made Lucia wish she could swoon like the heroine in a Victorian romance.

"No, please. I'm all right. Maybe I should go to

your place and clean out your kitchen instead. I think we still have your spare key."

"Absolutely not. I want you to go have fun at the party, and I promise I'll do my best to make it in time for trick or treat."

"I… thanks. I can't wait to see you."

"Me too. Now, make sure you eat a healthy breakfast before you go. I also want you to take an Uber. I'll bring you home."

"Yes, Daddy. I will."

"That's my sweet girl. It's gotten cold out, so you should wear street clothes for the trip, but I want you to bring that pretty pink dress for the party. I bet Princess Rainbow Kitty would like to go too."

Some people might have called his edicts micromanagement, but Lucia loved it. He made being little so easy, but also understood there was a grown woman inside her who could get an Uber for a ride into Manhattan, and arrange her own breakfast.

"I love you, Daddy."

"Oh, baby girl, I love you too. It makes me so happy to hear you say it." She heard more angry tapping of computer keys, and a low curse. "I'm sorry, but I need to get back to work so I can finish in time for trick or treat, okay?"

"I know. I'll see you soon."

"Bye, baby. Be a good girl for Daddy."

"Bye." The call dropped before the word was all the way out. Although she was sad he wouldn't be at the party, it was really for the littles. Daddies and mommies stayed on the sidelines until it was time for costumes and trick or treat.

It wasn't even trick or treat in the traditional sense. Instead of candy, the littles swarmed local businesses gathering canned goods for food pantries and shelters. It was fun and supported a great cause. Although she'd attended more than a few events as a chaperone, it would be the first time she'd participated as a little.

Surprisingly, she wasn't even nervous. Well, not very much. Coffee and a piece of toast with peanut butter helped to settle the butterflies dancing in her stomach much better than an omelet would have.

After arranging for an Uber, she went back upstairs and tucked her hair in a wrap, then took a quick shower and put on some mascara and lip gloss. Dressing in jeans, a cashmere sweater, and her favorite boots, she studied the contents of her little wardrobe and pulled out the pink dress, still bearing sales tags, plus her unicorn backpack. The frock went into the bag, along with cute black Mary Janes and some ribbons for her hair. Last, but not least, she laid Princess Rainbow Kitty on top and zipped it just as a horn blared from outside.

Unwilling to keep the driver waiting, she hurried out, nearly forgetting her jacket. The blustery breeze had her dashing back inside, and she giggled. Daddy would have spanked her for sure, and she'd almost forgotten her purse too. At least she'd remembered breakfast, and there was always a buffet of healthy, little-friendly snacks at the parties.

"Cold, isn't it?" the young woman behind the wheel asked when Lucia climbed in and buckled her seatbelt. "Yesterday was so nice."

"My…" *Daddy, sir, boyfriend, lover?* "…man took me to the zoo yesterday. It was the perfect day for it."

"That sounds amazing. I haven't been there in years." She eased her way into traffic. "I'm going to ask my boyfriend to take me next week before it gets too cold."

The driver's offhand comment made Lucia realize how much she'd been missing. She could have gone to the zoo at any time. Or the natural history museum, or any of a dozen other places in the city. She wanted to kick herself for being afraid for so long.

Lucia had the young woman drop her a half block away from the club to give herself time to get her head into little space. Although the clouds had cleared to reveal a blue sky and puffy clouds, the chilly breeze made her thankful to slide her member's keycard through the slot next to the unmarked door and get inside.

Mistress Candace, one of the owners, met her at the door. Dressed as always in a prim black suit with pearls, she was elegant and perfect.

"Good afternoon, Lucia." I'm glad you're here. One of our volunteers had a family emergency and couldn't make it. There are about thirty littles inside waiting for the party to start."

Lucia smiled and felt her face heat. She and Candace weren't close, but they'd always had a good working relationship and had collaborated on several successful projects. That was going to change now, and she didn't know what would happen.

"I…" She let out a breath, then said, "Can I talk to you privately?"

Mistress Candace's eyes widened imperceptibly at the sight of Lucia's unicorn backpack, and her lips twitched into a faint smile. "Of course. Let's go to my office."

Nodding her thanks, Lucia followed her down the hall leading away from the public areas of the club to a small, cramped office. Closing the door behind them, Lucia sat in the visitor's chair and looked down. "I'm… Well, I think maybe you won't be able to call on me to be a chaperone anymore."

"I wondered when you were going to come out," Candace murmured. "It sure took you long enough."

Her head coming up sharply, Lucia's mouth fell open. "You knew? Did Serena tell you?"

"I knew you and she weren't legally married. That was in your personnel file as a contractor for the club. I suspected the rest." She tapped a lacquered nail on her lower lip. "Besides, Serena would never have shared a confidence like that. If we didn't have a working relationship, I'd spank you myself for even suggesting it."

Leaning back, Lucia rubbed her face. "No, you're right. Serena wouldn't have done that. I'm sorry. I'm also sorry I won't be able to work as a domme anymore."

"Oh, I think there's still some domme inside you. It just won't be for the little events." Standing, she circled the desk and held out her hand. "You're welcome to do both, you know. As a switch, you're still one of the best educators out there."

Lucia took her hand and stood, shocked to silence when Candace pulled her into a hug.

"You don't mind?"

"Of course not. All I ask is that you keep an open mind about coming back as a domme." Tapping Lucia's nose, she added, "And not just a figurehead for parties. I want to see you out there beating someone's ass on occasion."

Laughing softly, Lucia nodded. "I can do that."

"Thank you. I'd have hated to give up one of my favorite dommes." Stepping past Lucia, she opened the door. "Go change into whatever pretty dress you have in that backpack. I'm assuming you don't have a Daddy yet, so I'll be vetting them before they approach you."

"Um... actually, I do. Ryan Sarver. He's working right now, but he should be here in time for trick or treat."

Candace snorted, her eyes sparkling with mirth. "You just broke the heart of every unattached sub in the city, but he's an excellent choice."

"Did you know about him too?"

"No, but I always thought he had the potential to be a very good daddy."

"He makes great teddy bear pancakes, and he took me to the zoo and got me a face painting and—"

They reached the locker room and Candace

swatted her butt. "Go get changed so you can join the party, little girl."

For once in her life, Lucia didn't fight against the fall into little space and changed into her pink dress after cutting off the tags. She had no idea why she'd expected judgment, but Candace's acceptance made her feel like anything was possible.

She fixed her hair into curly pigtails, then tucked Princess Rainbow Kitty under her arm. It was time to play.

CHAPTER 12

"*T*he backup is restored on the new server, and I replaced one of the power supplies to the system," Ryan said, drumming his fingers impatiently. He positioned his phone in the crook of his neck and continued coiling cables.

If Caroline asked him to stay until Monday, he was going to strangle her with her own pearls.

"Thank you. I suppose you can get on with the rest of your weekend, but I want you in bright and early Monday morning. I also trust there won't be a bill for—"

"Ms. Richards, I won't be in on Monday unless there's a problem I can't resolve remotely. Also, according to our contract, you are responsible for service calls outside regular business hours that are

164

longer than the two-hour maximum. I'm willing to deduct the rush shipping for the new server, but you will be paying for my time. The bill will be on your desk."

Without waiting for her to answer, he hung up and shook his head at Ebony. "Don't schedule that vacation you were planning to Aruba in January. We're not renewing the Richards contract."

"Thank God," she muttered, sending the invoice to her portable printer. "I was seriously thinking about quitting if you decided to sign another with that witch."

He glanced at his watch, scowling at the time. "Let's wrap things up and get out of here before she has time to land her broom."

"Hot date?" Ebony asked, packing up their tools.

He helped her with the trash and discarded packaging, making sure they left nothing behind. "You could say that." He hid a grin, imagining lifting Lucia's pretty pink dress over her hips to spank her lush ass.

"You go, boss. Whatever puts that sparkle in your eye is just fine by me."

"No idea what you're talking about," he muttered, pushing the button on the elevator. "What are your plans for the day?"

"I'm helping out with the Halloween party at my church, then trick or treating with the kids."

"Sounds fun." In fact, it was almost exactly what he'd be doing. Well, minus the church. Then again, there were plenty of people praying to God every Saturday night in Saints and Sinners. Giving her a wave, he got into his car, waiting until she drove away before he left.

Ryan sent a quick text to Lucia, letting her know he was on his way. Hopefully, she'd be too busy playing to get his message right away. He couldn't wait to see her having fun with her new friends.

After stopping by his condo for a shower and change of clothes, he drove back into Manhattan, hoping to catch the last hour of the party. The traffic Gods smiled upon him and he made it with time to spare.

When he swiped his keycard and opened the door, Mistress Candace nodded at him from behind the receptionist's podium. Angel, the young man who usually had that position, would be with his partner at the party.

"Hello, Daddy," she said, giving him a naughty smile. "Your baby girl is playing jump rope on the main stage, but we're short a couple of chaperones. Do you mind helping out?"

"Not at all." He studied her for a moment, then asked, "Are you okay with this?"

"Why wouldn't I be? You'll make a great daddy for Lucia. All I ask is that you allow her to be herself and let her be a domme when she needs to."

"She can be whatever she wants to be." Ryan leaned close, making sure Candace heard him. "But I won't tolerate you pushing her to domme when she wants to be a sub or a little."

"I knew there was a reason I liked you. Now, get out there before I remember you made a pretty good sub yourself."

"Ah, ah," he replied, waving a finger at her. "Baby dom in training doesn't count."

"It did when Serena had your dick in a cock cage and let me tease you."

"Naughty."

"You know it." Her smile softened and she sighed. "Go on, and congratulations. Serena would have been so proud of you both."

He coughed, swallowing the lump in his throat. "I like to think so too."

Giving her a nod, he opened the door leading into the main room and smiled at the noise of high-pitched giggles and squeals.

Instead of a well-equipped bondage club, the

space had been transformed into a playroom of a different sort. Colored streamers hung from the ceiling, along with balloons and glittery decorations. There was an inflated bouncy house and slide, hopscotch grids taped on the floor, pin the tail on the donkey, and a huge buffet laid out with snacks and a punchbowl. There was even a massive Lego table with bins full of blocks.

Ryan's fingers twitched. Legos had always been his jam, but he forced himself to stand still. He found Lucia almost immediately, her hair flying as she skipped a rope held by two women in frilly rompers.

One of her pigtails had come loose, sagging over her ear. Lips bowed into a wide smile, she was luminously beautiful. Her dress fluttered over lacy ruffled panties every time she jumped, and one of her knee socks had slid to her ankle. Princess Rainbow Kitty watched the festivities from a bench, surrounded by all manner of stuffies.

"Daddy!"

Lucia missed a jump and got tangled in the rope, nearly going sprawling. Her friends helped her up and she freed herself, then flew down the stairs. He opened his arms, setting his feet to catch her when she leaped into his arms and wrapped both legs around his hips.

"I missed you!" She peppered his face with kisses that smelled of candy corn and apples.

"Me too, baby girl." He squeezed her tight, then set her on her feet. "Go play with your friends. I'm going to help out with the Legos, okay?"

"Oooh, I love Legos!"

"Lucia, it's your turn to hold the rope!" one of the women called. "Come back and play!"

"Okay!" She jumped up to give him another kiss. "I want to play Legos with you later."

"I didn't know you liked them."

She blushed and tried to straighten her sock. "Why do you think I became an architect? I get paid for playing with buildings now."

"Lucia!"

Giving him one last kiss, she raced back up the stairs and took the end of the jump rope.

There was no question in his mind. Lucia was absolutely perfect.

LUCIA TOOK the end of the rope, grinning at her new friends, Sally and Becky. It was Sally's turn to jump, and Lucia hoped she didn't mess up. It was one thing to jump herself. She did it in the gym all the time, but wasn't sure she remembered how to turn the rope for someone else. It had been decades since elementary school.

Everyone had been so kind and patient. There were a few littles who had given her sideways glances at first, and a couple who had asked her to settle disputes. The volunteers stepped in and took care of the problems right away, giving her the chance to be a little.

The rhythmic click of rope against the floor lulled her into contemplative silence. Her fear had stifled her, and she'd lost out on so much. If she'd just grown a pair and tried, she could have had this all along. Even Candace had been welcoming, although Lucia knew she'd be expecting dominant Lucia back at some point.

That wasn't bad though. Lucia would only need to change her costume and her mindset, and Saints and Sinners would accept all of her. She didn't have to be just one thing anymore.

Told you so.

"Go away, weird inner voice," she muttered under her breath, frowning when Sally missed her step and crossed her legs, then ran to her.

"Mommy! I need to potty!"

Lucia smiled and pointed over Sally's shoulder at the woman trotting up the stairs.

Sally blinked and covered her eyes with her hands. "I'm so sorry, Lucia. That was completely rude."

"It's okay. It's my first day as a little. I'm still getting used to things too."

"You're doing great," Sally whispered. "I love your dress, and Princess Rainbow Kitty is perfect. Theodore Teddy loves her."

Becky nodded, her thumb drifting up to her mouth.

"Why don't we all go to the potty?" Sally's mommy asked. "I bet the three of you need to go after all that jumping."

Giggling, they followed Sally's mommy to the restroom. When they finished and washed up, Lucia waved them away so she could do something with her wrecked mass of hair. She wanted to look perfect for Ryan when she went back out.

Humming softly, she fixed her pigtails and pulled up her socks, then brushed the caramel popcorn crumbs from her dress.

Everyone was being so kind. A few people, mostly subs she'd had under her care in the past, were confused at first, but welcomed her with open arms. The masters and mistresses were just as generous, bringing her under their wings without missing a beat.

Best of all, Daddy didn't miss the party—just like he promised.

The door opened and closed softly, but she was too busy straightening her dress to see who it was.

"Still pretending to be a kid, I see."

She spun around, her belly clenching at the sound of the last voice in the world she wanted to hear.

Be brave, baby doll. He doesn't mean shit anymore.

Lucia straightened her spine, lifting her chin to face her douchebag ex-husband. "What are you doing here, Frank? This is a closed party."

Time hadn't treated him well. He'd never been one to take care of himself, and looked at least a decade older than his years. It wasn't even his age or unhealthy appearance. It was the mean look in his eyes. She shuddered, thanking her lucky stars she'd gotten out.

He stalked closer, getting into her space. "I saw your photo on the club website and thought we might talk." He sneered, giving her a once over with cold blue eyes. "I was hoping you'd have gotten help for your psychosis by now."

"I'm not getting into this with you." She stepped around him, crying out when he grabbed her arm and slammed her against the wall.

"See, I'm thinking I made a mistake. I should have beaten you more often and broken you of wanting to be a little. Don't you realize how sick you are?"

"Let me go, asshole!" She jerked away, but he caught her hair, tugging her head back.

"Despite your mental deficiency, you've done well. I saw that big house you're living in. Who did you fuck to get it?" He leaned close, his warm breath on her neck making her throat tighten. "Is he just as crazy as you are?"

"Did you give up gambling, Frank?" she snapped, slamming her elbow into his chest. Gasping for air, he backed up, his eyes widening with surprise. "How's your credit rating these days? Did you find some other poor woman to mooch off of?"

"You utter bitch!" He swung at her, making her duck.

The door opened, but she didn't dare take her eyes off Frank. "Is that why you're here?" she taunted, praying her knees held her up. "Come to look for another sugar mama? How's that working out for you?"

"Mommy! Lucia's in trouble!"

Sally's panicked scream filled her with sorrow. She should never have come here as a little. It caused nothing but trouble, and now she'd ruined the party.

Frank was right about one thing. She didn't fit anywhere. A little couldn't exist in a domme's body. She'd always fight with both sides of her nature, and couldn't expect anyone else to deal with her issues. She wanted to cry, knowing it would cost her Ryan. He wanted a baby girl, not a domme.

Seconds later, the room filled with angry men, all focused on Lucia's ex-husband. Ryan pushed his way through the crowd and swept her into his arms.

"Disgusting," Frank shouted, slapping at the hands holding him still. "You're just as sick as she is."

"Did he hurt you, baby girl?" Ryan asked, ignoring Frank.

She wanted to bury her face in Ryan's chest and sob her heart out. He was a daddy, and would try to make everything better, but he couldn't.

Frank had ruined everything, but he'd brought a very important truth home. Thinking she could be a little had been a horrible mistake. All of it. And now it was time to fix it.

"No. I'm fine." She took a deep breath, then added, "Let me down, please. I need to finish this."

He let her go and she gave him one last hug

before turning to face her ex-husband. "You're entitled to your opinion," she said softly, letting her domme self take control. "But you are not going to come into *my* place and spout your judgmental bullshit all over everyone else. You're going to be escorted out now, and I'm going to make damned sure you're blackballed from every club in the city."

"Really? What do you think you're going to do?"

"Don't test me," she snapped. "There are dozens of witnesses here, all of whom are going to share this story. You can leave now and try to save your dignity, or you're going to find out just how much power I have."

"Fucking bitch," he muttered.

Thankfully, he let the dungeon monitors show him out, leaving her to face the aftermath of some very poor decisions.

Long live Mistress Lucia. Hail to the domme.
Goodbye, baby doll.

CHAPTER 13

"*D*on't do it, Ryan," Candace warned as Frank was escorted out. "You have a baby girl to take care of, and he isn't worth it."

"Maybe." He supposed his need to beat Frank to a pulp was clear on his face. "It would make me feel a lot better."

"Lucia is all you need to be thinking about right now," she countered, jerking her head at the bathroom door.

It opened, revealing Lucia dressed in street clothes instead of her pink party dress. The adorable pigtails were gone and her hair was wrapped in a black scarf. Shadows darkened the skin under her beautiful brown eyes. The door shut behind her and she dropped her unicorn backpack in the trash can just outside, then gave him a watery smile.

"Hey," she murmured, walking toward him. "We need to talk."

There was a perceptible difference between little Lucia and domme Lucia, and it had nothing to do with the clothes she wore. She wasn't cold, but there was a decided set to her shoulders and jaw that changed her entire persona. There was nothing left of her submissive side, and he wanted to rage at the loss.

Pressing a keycard into his hand, Candace whispered, "Use the classroom on the mezzanine level. I'll get her bag."

He nodded and moved to Lucia, taking her hand. "Let's go upstairs."

"All right." She tried to extricate herself from his grip, but he refused to let go, forcing her to walk with him.

The classroom was exactly as it was named. There was a blackboard, a teacher's desk, and a half dozen small tables and chairs for students. A small cupboard in the corner housed impact implements to chastise naughty bottoms. Maps covered the walls, along with art created by littles who enjoyed this space.

It was an exact replica of the classroom in Club Apocalypse, a very popular resort just east of Winslow, Arizona. Built in a renovated vintage motel by four military retirees who called themselves the Four Horsemen, it was a mecca of kink with a world-class dungeon and dining facilities set in a hundred acres of desert.

There would be time to think about taking her there later.

"Have a seat," he ordered, pointing at one of the student tables.

"I think that was my line," she replied, propping a hip on the corner of the teacher's desk. "You're messing up my heartfelt breakup, so I'm just going to get to the point."

"We're not breaking up," he replied, standing in front of her. He was invading her space, but he wasn't about to let her off so easily.

"Oh?" She sighed and shook her head. "Things aren't going to work with us, Ryan. Aside from that, we were never really together in the first place."

"How do you figure?" He put his hands on her shoulders, moving to stand between her thighs. "You made friends. Everything was going well until your asshole ex showed up."

"That's the point." She stood and shook him off,

then crossed the room. "He's an asshole, but he was right about something. Everyone assumes I'm a domme. I was asked more than once to break up disputes, and one of the littles asked me to take her to the bathroom."

"So? It's only been a few hours. You have to give them time."

She bit her lip and moved to the door. "Face it, honey. You can't turn a sow's ear into a silk purse. I'm never going to be accepted as a little, and I've destroyed my credibility as a domme."

"I don't accept that."

Her shoulders lifted into a shrug and she opened the door. "That's your choice, but I'm not going to hold a grudge when you find someone who will fit with you better."

Blocking her way, Ryan made her focus on him instead of the exit. "What happened to loving me?" he demanded. "Was that just something to say during sex?"

He regretted the words the minute they came out, but it was too late. Lucia's face hardened into remote implacability. "Fuck you, Ryan. I'm out."

She left, her booted footsteps loud on the metal treads.

"Lucia, wait!" he shouted, to no avail. She flipped him off and continued down the stairs.

"Shit!" He slammed his fist into the wall, cracking the plaster and raising bloody cuts on his knuckles. "What do I do now, Serena?" he demanded. "You've been all up my ass for the entire weekend, so tell me what to do!"

No one gave him an answer. Ryan hadn't expected one though. He'd fucked things up, and it was time to either give up or figure out another way to get through to Lucia.

Giving up wasn't an option. He loved her, and couldn't bear the thought of losing her. He just didn't know how to make things right after screwing things up so badly.

Maybe you should have said that first, baby dom.

Great. "It would have been helpful if you'd have said something before. Go away and quit haunting me."

It wasn't just him. Saints and Sinners was a community, and the loss of Lucia would hit everyone. She was an icon, just as Serena had been. Maybe it needed to be more than him. Lucia had to see her presence meant something.

Glancing around the classroom, he prayed for

inspiration, his gaze focusing on a roll of white butcher paper and a bin of art supplies. Grabbing everything, he went downstairs.

"Ladies, littles, and gentlemen," he announced. "I need your help."

LUCIA'S PHONE started chiming with text messages from Ryan before she was a block away. Scowling, she turned it off and shoved it in her purse. Instead of calling for another Uber, Lucia hiked six blocks to Central Park. Her boots were comfortable, but she missed her pretty light-up sneakers.

Just as well. She had every intention of tossing them into the trash, along with the contents of her little bedroom. After that, she'd put the brownstone on the market and move into a condo. It was too much space for one person.

She sat on a bench, smiling sadly at the pigeons landing near her feet in hopes of a handout. Maybe it was time to leave New York altogether. Job offers came in all the time. One particularly attractive one in California would double her net income.

One brave bird pecked at her boot, glaring at her.

"Sorry, buddy. No snacks here," she murmured. It flew away, quick to give up on her.

It was getting too cold to sit, and the sun was going down. Children in costumes played in the park, watched over by parents and nannies. She'd missed out on trick or treat too.

Letting out a sigh, she got to her feet and left the park. She'd eaten too much junk food to bother with supper, but stopped at a street cart for an order of falafel with spicy yogurt sauce, devouring the yummy fried goodness while she walked.

"Five dollars for a fortune!" a busker called. "I'll tell you the future for five dollars, pretty lady."

Lucia stopped and handed the woman a twenty. "Barstow, Baton Rouge, or Branson?"

"Give me your hand."

Smiling, Lucia rolled her eyes and obeyed. "This is more fun than throwing a dart at a map."

"Hush."

Aged hands wrapped around hers, surprisingly warm as the woman looked up to reveal sightless eyes that didn't quite meet Lucia's face. "Barstow, but you won't be alone. Don't forget your daddy."

"Um… Okay, thank you." Lucia tried to step back, but the woman held on and pushed the bill toward her.

"No charge," she murmured. "I almost never get an actual real vision. You should get a pedicure first so you can wear sandals."

"That's just fucked up."

Letting Lucia go, the woman smiled and said, "Probably, but I hear the weather is better than New York's. Enjoy California, baby doll."

"Yeah." Lucia shivered, then strode away. "Always some fuckery in Gotham on Halloween," she muttered. "Total bullshit."

There was only one person in the world who called Lucia baby doll. And she was six feet under.

She spotted a cab and flagged it down, wanting nothing more than to go home. Everything reminded her of Ryan or Serena, and she wasn't having it.

Passing by MOMA made her cringe. The lions in front of the public library gave her accusing stares.

He'd take his new little girl to those places. It wasn't going to be her—especially after what he said. He could have told her he loved her, but no. He'd accused her of saying it in the heat of the moment.

She almost hated him for that, and for showing her how good it could be before yanking it all away.

Fuck him sideways and endways.

"Drop me at the end of the bridge, please?" she asked.

"You got it." He pulled off into Main Street Park, then handed her a white business card with a suicide prevention hotline number in large black text. "Baby doll, the East River is too gangster for a pretty lady like you."

"Why did you call me that?" Lucia asked, her fingers tightening on the door handle.

He turned to look at her, dreads falling in his face. "I have no idea, but I really want to take you home instead of leaving you here."

Lucia gave him the card, then leaned back against the seat. "I'm not going to jump. I just wanted to look at the water."

"There's a full moon tonight, baby doll, but it sure is pretty. Want some company?"

"Turn the meter off?"

He laughed and got out, holding the door for her. "I got a bottle of tequila under the seat. Want some?"

"Yeah."

They walked to the center of the bridge, ignoring the traffic whizzing by. It was comforting, this absolute stranger, a man she'd never met, but who cared enough to talk.

She took a pull from the bottle and handed it back, marveling at the silvery moon reflected on the slow-moving river. "I got ninety-nine problems."

"Tell me about it," he muttered. "I got me six kids, and my wife left me. What's your story, baby doll?"

"I got me a man who told me he loved me during sex. I said it back, then he…"

She couldn't say it out loud, but the cabbie saved her from responding.

"That ain't cool. What you gonna do?"

"I'm moving to California."

"Better weather." He tipped the bottle to his lips, then capped it. "Ready to go home?"

"That's what the fortune teller across from Central Park said," she muttered, following him back to the cab.

"Don't mean she's wrong," he retorted.

She got in and fastened her seatbelt, inhaling the scent of old cab and citrusy aftershave. "You're a good man."

"Name's Anton."

"Lucia."

He double parked in front of her brownstone and turned in his seat. "It's been a pleasure, baby doll. Hit me up if you come back to the city."

"Thanks." She got out, then leaned down to kiss his cheek, pressing several bills into his hand. "For the ride and the conversation. Be well, Anton."

"You too, Lucia." He waited until she mounted the steps and opened her door, then drove away.

CHAPTER 14

*W*here the hell was Lucia?

Ryan was worried sick. She'd been gone for hours and wasn't answering her phone. He was half tempted to call the cops, but they wouldn't do anything for a grown woman missing less than a day.

A key turned in the lock and he breathed out a sigh of relief, then stepped from the kitchen. Looking disheveled and windblown, Lucia came inside, then hung up her coat.

Dropping her purse on the occasional table, she moved into the living room and blinked, spinning around to see what he'd done.

"Holy shit."

"It's all true," he said, resisting the urge to pull her into his arms. "Everyone wrote something."

He'd made sure of it. There was at least fifty yards of butcher paper hung around the room with drawings and scribbled well-wishes from littles and subs, plus all the dominants and people she'd helped along the way. It covered the walls, and he'd laid it over furniture when he ran out of space.

"I see that." Striding to the wall, she started pulling the paper down, balling it up as she went. "Thanks for the thought. I'm sure you can see yourself out."

"I'm not going anywhere." He put his hands around her waist and lifted her off her feet, then sat on the couch, holding her firmly in his lap. "We're going to sit here until you listen to me."

"What happened to consent?"

"Consent only happens after you hear what I have to say."

Muttering profanities under her breath, she struggled for a few seconds, then gave up with an irritated sigh. "Fine. Speak your piece, then get out."

"First, I have a question. Do you still love your ex-husband?"

"Of course not! What kind of question is that?" She wriggled again, giving him a furious glare when he cuddled her more firmly against his chest and didn't let go.

"I had to ask because you seem very concerned about what he thinks. If you don't have feelings for him, why do you care?"

"I don't care," she snapped. "He's an asshole."

"Then I'd like you to explain why you thought his opinion meant more than that of people who love you."

"You accused me of using that word in a moment of passion," she countered. "Why are you throwing it out there now?"

Her lower lip went out in a cute little pout, meaning she was about to get stubborn. Well, more stubborn than she already was. Ryan was glad to see it though. It meant her little was still in there, still needing to come out.

"I'm sorry. I was wrong, and I should have never said that. I should have told you I love you no matter what."

Sighing heavily, she rubbed her eyes. She looked so damned tired, and all he wanted to do was spank her for scaring him, then tuck her into bed with him and Princess Rainbow Kitty. Speaking of whom...

"I almost forgot," he said, pulling the toy from

behind a throw pillow. "You left Princess Rainbow Kitty behind."

Her hand shaking, she took it from him and buried her face in the plush fabric. Ryan let out a sigh of relief. He'd been half afraid she'd refuse it, which would have broken his heart. He couldn't let her bury her little even deeper.

"Do you think I'm mentally ill?" she asked, her voice muffled in faux fur.

"Is that what your ex told you?" When she nodded, he tipped up her chin to make her look at him. "The only one who needs help is him. What right does he have to judge people for how they live their lives?"

"But he said—"

"Does it matter?" Ryan wiped a glistening tear from the corner of her eye. "We've already established you don't care what he thinks, so I'm going to ask you why his words hit you so hard. Why did they make you feel bad about yourself?"

"Because deep down, I still believe it. And you said you wanted a baby girl, but how can I be that when I'm so torn about what I am?"

He let her free, knowing she needed the space to get her thoughts together. "Seems to me you have a very good idea about who and what you are."

She spun to face him and laughed harshly. "How can you even say that? I have no idea how I'm going to wake up in the morning most days. Will I be little, or sub, or domme? Do you know how exhausting that is?"

"It's exhausting because you're fighting," he said gently.

"You have no frame of reference, Ryan. I appreciate you trying to help, but this just isn't going to work."

"Actually, I do." Reaching out, he caught her and pulled her back into his lap, sending up a prayer of thanks when she didn't fight. "I lived here as a sub for two weeks. I slept on the floor at the foot of the bondage bed. I cooked your food, did your laundry, ironed your clothes, and submitted to you and Serena completely."

"But you wanted that." She blanched and a horrified expression crossed her face. "Please, don't tell me we violated your consent. We asked every day, but—"

"No. You absolutely did not violate my consent, Lucia." He hugged her tight to make sure she got the message. "It was part of my training, and I accepted that knowing it would be difficult."

"Thank goodness." Her body softened and she let

out a sigh of relief. "How do you think this applies to me?"

"I'm not a sub, baby girl. I know what you're feeling because every single morning I had to force myself out of my dominant mindset and take on that role. It was exhausting, but then I stopped fighting it."

"I don't understand."

He leaned back against the cushions and encouraged her to put her head on his shoulder. "Being submissive to you and Serena wasn't going to lessen my dominance. All I had to do was remember why I was there. It was one step toward learning to be a better dom."

"That doesn't really apply to me though. We all knew what you were doing."

"The internal battle was the same." Ryan kissed her temple and rested his cheek against her head. "I'm not lessening your struggle, Lucia. There are three parts of you demanding attention. All I'm saying is maybe you could try letting them out instead of forcing yourself to fit someone else's mold."

Closing her eyes, she sat silently for several seconds. "What would you have done if I wasn't feeling little today?"

"We'd have done something else, or we could have gone as chaperones. I'm pretty adaptable that way."

"But you shouldn't have to be." She lifted her head and kissed his cheek, then moved to sit next to him on the couch. "I really appreciate you trying to make me feel better, but I think I'd rather just end this before you get tired of dealing with my crap."

He let out a breath, then stood and walked to the fireplace. He couldn't look at her without wanting to shake some sense into her. "You're not even willing to meet me halfway, are you?"

"I care about you a lot, but I just don't think it's in either of our best interest."

Turning to face her, he nodded, trying to keep his face an emotionless mask. "All right, but do me a favor and think about what I said. It might not be me, but you're going to have to let someone in sooner or later. Just… Don't let your fear make you chase them away."

She choked out a sob and sniffed. "I'm really sorry," she whispered.

"Me too." His feet dragging, he walked out.

THE FRONT DOOR closed behind him.

Swallowing hard, she raced for the bathroom, barely making it before all the junk she'd eaten at the party made a reappearance. Knowing Ryan wouldn't be back was the absolute worst feeling in the world. Tears streamed from her eyes and she curled up on the bathroom floor, sobbing her heart out.

Her head aching, she finally sat up and used a washcloth to clean up her face.

She was letting fear rule her life. But she was afraid of so much more than what people thought of her. Losing Ryan felt awful, but would have been a thousand times worse if their relationship had gotten a chance to flourish.

They'd had two days of absolute perfection. A whole weekend of a fantasy of what her life might have looked like where all the pieces of her fit together with someone else.

Someone who loved her.

Pinching the bridge of her nose to hold back another crying jag, she went into the kitchen for a glass of wine. It was perfectly clean, but Ryan had already set up her coffeepot, and put out her favorite mug for the morning.

Sighing, she opened the fridge and lost it all over again at the sight of all the food he'd obviously purchased while she was traipsing across Manhattan. He'd even replaced her chocolate stash and bought fresh dinosaur marshmallows, along with a few boxes of sugary cereal she almost never ate.

The unicorn backpack she'd thrown into the trash at Saints and Sinners sat on the breakfast bar.

"Lucia, you are a massive dumbass."

It was her own voice, but she was pretty sure her inner bitch was saying the same thing.

Worse, it was her own stupid fault Ryan was gone. If she'd just had a little faith, and some lady balls, maybe things would have worked out. He was right about everything.

Still crying, she made her way upstairs, but her feet stalled. She didn't want to sleep in her little bedroom, and her grownup bedroom wasn't an option. It would be awhile before she could go into that room without thinking of the night she'd shared with Ryan.

That left the bondage bed in the playroom, the couch, or...

She opened the door to Serena's bedroom, wishing she'd gotten it cleaned out. After stripping down to her panties, she crawled between the slightly musty sheets, then pulled the spare pillow into her belly and turned off the lamp on the nightstand. Closing her eyes, she tried to sleep, wishing she'd thought to bring her night light from the other room.

"You really are a massive dumbass," Serena's voice said.

"You're dead. Go away."

"No. You're in my bed. That means you will listen to my pep talk."

Groaning, Lucia rolled over. "Fine. Say what you have to say, then go away."

"Okay. I'm short on time, and I'm not supposed to be here, so you're getting the *too long didn't read* version. Get your ass out of bed and get dressed. Call a cab and go to Ryan. Tell him how you feel. Get down on your knees and beg him for another chance. You will also stop being a fucking moron, baby doll."

Lucia jerked awake and shot out of bed, absolutely certain Serena had been in the room. Aside from the faint scent of faded perfume, there was no evidence anyone had been there.

"That's your idea of a pep talk?" she shouted. "Quit haunting me!"

Grabbing her jeans and shirt, she dressed, then called a cab, hoping to get Anton again. "I might not have been crazy before, but now I'm talking to a dead woman," she muttered, pulling on her boots.

Serena, or more likely her subconscious, was right. Lucia couldn't be happy without her daddy, and she wasn't about to sit around waiting for him to come back. She had to meet him halfway this time, and go even further. Nothing else would do but complete surrender.

Ryan was her daddy. She had to stop and let him be that for her. Maybe things wouldn't work, but Lucia wouldn't know until she tried. Locking the door behind her, she tapped her foot impatiently, praying the cab would show up.

To her relief, it rounded the corner and pulled to a stop. "Hey, baby doll. Need a lift?" Anton called through the open window.

"Yeah." She ran down the stairs and flung herself into the back seat, rattling off Ryan's address in a breathless voice. "I need to be in the Bronx yesterday."

"What's the rush?" He turned around, then hit the gas. "You running from someone?"

"No. I'm running *to* someone. I've got to eat some crow, apologize, and do that big romcom grand gesture thing before he realizes I'm a bad bet."

"Whoa," Anton said, speeding up. "What brought this on?"

She let out a slightly hysterical laugh. "The ghost of Halloween present has been haunting my dumb ass all weekend."

He gave her a dubious glance in the mirror, then shrugged. "Can I watch? I need some happy ever after in my life."

"Sure, but we're going to fade to black before you see the naughty bits."

He chuckled then slowed for a traffic light. "Dang, no fair."

Smiling, she turned to look out the window. The full moon bathed the city in an eerie silver glow, but it was gorgeous. It was almost as if the universe was approving her decision.

A car coming the other way slowed and parked across the street. The door opened, and her breath stalled when Ryan stepped from the vehicle.

"Stop!"

Anton slammed on the brakes, then shouted after her when she got out and darted across the street, nearly getting creamed by a garbage truck. She ignored the blaring horns and skidded to a stop in front of Ryan.

Dropping to her knees, she peered up at him. "I

love you. You were right. I'm terrified out of my wits, but I'm sorry. I want to—"

"Baby girl, what are you doing out so late? And what possessed you to run in front of a garbage truck?" he asked, helping her to her feet.

"Baby doll, not baby girl!" Anton shouted.

"Who is that?"

Blushing, she hid her face in her hands and tried not to giggle. "He's my cabbie, Anton."

"Make with the happy ever after! I have another fare to pick up."

He blinked and smiled wryly. "Okay, then. Why are you out so late?"

"I was coming to see you."

"Funny, I was coming to see you too. Now, calm down and tell me again what you were trying to say, then I'm going to take you home and spank your ass for playing in traffic."

"I…" She inhaled and tried to slow her racing heart. "I love you, Ryan Sarver. I want to be your baby girl, and your everything else too."

"Even though you're scared?"

"Especially because I'm scared." She rested her head on his chest and wrapped her arms around him, thanking all the gods she could think of that he allowed it. "You're my daddy and you always know what to do when I'm afraid."

"Honey, I don't just want your little," he replied, cupping her jaw. "I want you in my collar. I want to assist you when you top a sub. I want everything, because I love you more than anything. Are you ready to give it to me?"

She hugged him tighter. "I'm ready, Daddy. Can my collar have a kitten on it?"

"Thank fuck," he murmured. Picking her up, he tossed her over his shoulder, then stalked down the street. "You can have whatever you want, but you're going to get that spanking I promised first."

Giggling, she reached down and pinched Ryan's butt, earning herself a sharp spank for her trouble. Everything was going to be perfect, and she didn't even care that her tummy was going to be sore if he kept bouncing her around.

Anton's cab followed them slowly and he honked his horn. "Is this a happy ever after?" he shouted.

"Go away, Anton!" Ryan retorted. "We'll invite you to the wedding."

Laying on his horn, Anton drove into the night.

"You should let me down now," Lucia said. "I'm not going to run away ever again."

He spanked her once more, but let her slide to

her feet. Cupping her cheeks, he kissed her, stealing her breath. By the time he lifted his head, her knees were weak with desire.

"Even if you do, I'm going to chase you, baby. I'll never let you go."

"I'm counting on it. I love you, Daddy."

EPILOGUE

hat was time to an angel?

It wasn't as if she'd be receiving wings anytime soon. She had an abundance of that precious commodity. Serena shuffled the pages of Lucia and Ryan's file into order, laying them neatly in front of her. If they turned into the rainbows of happily ever after…

When—not if. There was no question Ryan and Lucia would have their true love, and that first spark would be glorious.

"I thought I might find you here."

Warmth covered her shoulder and Serena rested her cheek on Lucifer's clawed hand. Perhaps it was strange to accept comfort from the prince of darkness, but she didn't care.

"Am I so predictable?" she asked, lifting her head to meet his red eyes. "I'm surprised to see you."

In a voice like gravel over silk, he laughed. "I go where I please." Stroking a callused finger over her jaw, he added, "Much like women and cats."

She didn't bother trying to hide the shiver his touch brought forth. He was too observant. "Quoting Robert Heinlein? How... nerdy."

"What can I say? He's fun at parties. You're here because you wait for proof your charges found their happily ever after, just as other guardians have done for thousands of years." He rested a hip on the arm of her chair, then bent close, his lips brushing the shell of her ear. "You could go see for yourself, little one. All you have to do is accept me."

It was a shame Lucifer was such an asshole. He really was too sexy for words. He knew perfectly well she was bound until Gabriel assigned her to another task. She couldn't leave unless she did the unthinkable and agreed to Lucifer's offer of sanctuary.

The idea held a certain appeal. What better place for a dominatrix than an entire hell realm filled with penitents in desperate need of punishment? Really, pink wings would not suit her at all. Unfortunately, there were still too many people requiring guidance on Earth for her to act so selfishly, not the least of whom was Mitchell Sakurai.

His time was measured, and the weight of it pressed down on her with foreboding.

And that lovely cab driver could use her personal touch as well.

Tick tock, Gabriel. Let's move things along, shall we?

"My name is Madame Serena," she retorted, scowling. "I'm nobody's little one, nor am I a toy for your amusement."

"And that is my greatest disappointment. I could make you beg to kneel at my feet." Lucifer tipped her chin up until their lips were scant millimeters apart, then bared a hint of fang. "Alas my—"

A flash of lightning lit up the office and Gabriel appeared, his face red with fury.

"—my dear brother has come to spoil our fun."

Lucifer brushed his lips across hers. His scent of ambergris and wood smoke made her belly clench with need, but she pushed the inconvenient response away, wishing she could move Lucifer aside with equal aplomb.

Gabriel tightened his hands into fists and inhaled through his nose. Serena crossed her legs and leaned back in the chair behind his desk, letting her favorite red Manolo pump dangle from a swinging foot.

"You went too far," he spat, slamming his palms down on the desk. "How dare you?"

"To whom are you speaking?" she asked calmly. "Me or Lucifer?"

"You!" Gabriel shouted. "You dare invite Lucifer into heaven and sit in my chair like you have the right. On no fewer than a dozen occasions, you've risked exposing yourself to your human. You've violated their minds with your thoughts and imposed your will upon them without considering the consequences. You've—"

The files on her dear Lucia and Ryan flew into the air and swirled, then exploded into a thousand shards of rainbow-colored light. Serena breathed out a sigh of relief. It was one thing to know it would happen, but quite another to see the evidence for herself.

Lucifer plucked her from the chair and swung her into his arms, spinning her around. "See, darling? I knew we could do it!"

We?

That was enough of that. She was absolutely done with people telling her how to think, how to feel, what to do, and how to manage her charges.

"Darling, do be a good little fallen angel and toddle off back to Hell, please," she said, her voice thick with saccharine acid. "Otherwise, I might have to see if I can use my angelic magic to lock your junk in a cock cage until you learn to mind your manners."

Drawing himself up to his full height, Lucifer glowered, then disappeared as quickly as he'd come.

"Well," Gabriel said, sitting across from her. "That was interesting." A small smile played across his lips, but he quickly smoothed it away.

"I didn't invite him, if that's what you're wondering." Serena stood and rounded the desk separating them, then propped her hip on the edge. "Nor did he assist me in any fashion."

"Be that as it may, you broke so many rules, I can't allow you to take responsibility for another human, Serena." Gabriel rubbed his face and sighed. "You have to see the position I'm in."

"Actually, I don't." Reaching across the desk, she dragged the massive tome containing guardian lore toward them. "Show me where it says I can't pretend to be their wiser inner voice."

"I fail to see—"

"I read it, Gabriel. Cover to cover. I can't allow humans to see me, directly influence their choices, or force a bond that won't end in true love. There are over a thousand pages of allegory and case study that belabor those three tenets."

In Gabriel's defense, she *had* gone a little too far with Lucia in giving her those last marching orders to get her on her feet and where she belonged.

"That isn't the point."

"Then what is?" she asked, honestly curious. "Is it me you have a problem with, or is it my methods?"

Instead of answering, he gritted his teeth and looked away for a moment, then said, "It's not you, per se. It's just all my guardians are looking for true love for their charges now. They're not doing the little things."

"You'll have to explain that to me. I'm afraid I'm not following."

He took the book and opened it to a spot about a third of the way through, then turned it toward her. "Have you heard of the butterfly effect?" he asked, pointing at a page of text.

"Yes, of course. A butterfly beats its wings, causing a breeze that creates a storm, and so forth."

"Indeed." Gabriel peered at her, his gaze solemn and intent. "You should read this. You might not have noticed, but it pertains to you, personally."

Pressing her lips together with annoyance, Serena read the page, her hands tightening into fists at the end. "Do you mean to tell me I died because a woman got a flat tire on the Manhattan Bridge at rush hour?"

"No," Gabriel said gently. "You died because her guardian quietly urged her to hurry to her lover instead of having her tire checked. She wrecked her car, and the ambulance sent to help you couldn't get through the traffic jam. Two women died because of one guardian's poor decision."

Serena straightened and looked up at the shards of paper still floating down from the ceiling, then huffed out a dry laugh. "Well, that's... prosaic?"

No, it was irritating as hell, but there wasn't much she could do about it. She was more aggravated at herself for not fully understanding the meaning of all those stories. She'd never been a fan of allegory, and after the first few hundred, they all started to run together.

"I'm sorry if it upset you," Gabriel murmured. "But I hope you see my position."

"It's fine. I get it." She chewed on her lower lip, then stood. "I'm going to help you rewrite this into something everyone can understand without wading through thousands of pages."

"You mean to throw away the lore of millennia?" he demanded, his face flat with anger.

"No, but if I didn't get the point from reading it, do you think anyone else will? Do you think maybe that's why the other guardians are looking for that ridiculous points payout and not focusing on those little things? You've set the whole thing up to reward them for doing exactly that."

"What do you suggest?"

Gabriel still didn't look entirely happy, but Serena was running out of patience. "One page. Boil everything down into... you know what? Make your own commandments. Ten of them that outline exactly what you want guardians to do."

"That's not nearly enough!"

"Distill it," she retorted. Her voice softening, she laid a hand on his arm. "I said I would help, and I will, but I want something in return."

"You want Mitchell Sakurai."

"Yes. I promise I won't even look for a true love for him, but I won't stop it if it happens on its own. Deal?"

"Deal." He gave her a sideways glance, then added, "You know, you would make a most excellent queen of Hell. Perhaps you should give my brother a chance."

Serena shook her head, but chuckled with wry

amusement. "Probably, but not until Lucifer bows to me. We both know he'll never do that."

"As you say." Giving her a wink, he pulled out a notepad and a pen. "Shall we get to work?"

Thanks for reading! Turn the page for an exciting excerpt from Zinnia's Solstice Daddy, the next Holiday Daddy Dom.

For sneak peeks and teasers, sign up for my newsletter. You'll also get a free book delivered right to your inbox!

ZINNIA'S SOLSTICE DADDY

SNEAK PEEK

*S*erena followed the line of soldiers, keeping an eye on Mitchell Sakurai. As usual, he was in the front, too dominant and protective to give up his most dangerous position.

Armored clothing the color of the surrounding mountains covered him from head to toe, hiding his lean body. The face shield on his helmet revealed a hint of the thick black beard he'd grown, but concealed his remarkable light brown eyes.

If she had to pick a favorite out of all her toys, it would have been Mitchell. A master rigger even before coming to her for lessons, he was quiet and reserved, yet had a dry wit she enjoyed. She'd never tell a soul, but he was the only one with whom she'd developed a relationship beyond that of teacher and student. He'd become a friend, and the only person she trusted to give her advice about managing her dear Lucia's little.

Of course, now that Lucia and Ryan had each other, she could move on to helping Mitchell.

She might or might not have told Gabriel a slight fib. Although she wanted to keep Mitchell breathing and safe, she also wanted to help him find that special little girl who would complete him. He never played with the same sub twice, meaning his relationships were shallow and temporary at best. It was irritating to a woman who wanted a happily ever after for everyone.

"Testosterone poisoning," Lucifer muttered, taking her arm to help her over a chunk of fallen rock. "Traipsing through these mountains wanting to be heroes."

"I thought you'd be happy with this location. All this war must be filling Hell with souls quite nicely."

"Bah." His face reddened and he scowled. "You'd be surprised at how few there are."

"Oh? Why did you come, then?"

She hurried forward, her Manolo pumps gliding over loose rock and scree. All these mountains filled with blind spots and caves made her nervous for Mitchell, and the fiercely biting wind made it impossible to hear anything. She didn't have time to focus on her unwanted companion.

"Is it so impossible to believe it's for your charming company?" he countered.

"Considering I offered to lock you in male chastity the last time we spoke, yes, I'm afraid it is."

"So distrustful." He was suddenly at her back and pulled her to a stop, his arms wrapped loosely around her hips. "I simply wanted to see what you find so attractive about this unpleasant duty."

"We've discussed this before," she murmured. It did no good to wriggle free. He'd simply come back like a bad penny. It was an utter shame she liked it. Lucifer made her feel like there was someone out there who understood her. Her brand of love wasn't kind or gentle. She wanted rough and dirty, and she wanted to hurt people.

And sometimes, she wanted to see them bleed for it.

She never revealed herself, knowing her kinks went beyond appropriate levels of safe and sane. Yet Lucifer accepted those darker desires and welcomed them.

It didn't help that she wanted him badly. Thankfully, neither of them was willing to compromise, so there was no hope of anything happening between them.

If it ever did, they'd set the cosmos on fire.

"I want Mitchell to be safe and find happiness."

"I didn't realize you harbored such altruism."

"Hardly. Sadistic dominatrix, remember?"

He grunted and let her pull away to follow the line of soldiers. "Yet you're still out here following cannon fodder into an ambush."

"What?" Horrified, she spun to face him. "Where?"

There was no way she could protect all of Mitchell's men. To do so would mean revealing her presence, and she'd promised Gabriel she wouldn't break any of the new guardian commandments they'd hammered out. She wouldn't be able to protect Mitchell either, considering he'd be the first in the line of fire.

Lucifer lifted a negligent hand. "About half a mile ahead. Not far now." Stepping closer, he drew a claw over the curve of her jaw. "I might be willing to help you keep them safe though."

"Thank you," she breathed. "Can we turn them around somehow? What do we need to do?"

"All you have to do is accept a gift from me, lovely angel. I have in my possession the men who shot all those women and children in that Kabul maternity hospital. I will gift them to you. They will receive the punishment they deserve at your expert hands, and Mitchell will remain alive and able to find the true love you so want for him."

Serena should have known better. Lucifer never gave anything away for free. Still, unfettered access to the men who had committed that horrifying crime against humanity was very tempting. Thinking of all the things she'd do to them made her heart beat faster with cruel anticipation.

There was no such thing as a safe word in Hell.

"In exchange for what?"

"Such a simple thing," he murmured, brushing his lips over hers. "Kneel for me, darling. Accept this as your last assignment as a guardian angel and agree that I will forever be your lord and master."

"Did you set this up?" she hissed. "Did you arrange for Mitchell to walk into a trap?"

"No, but I probably would have if I'd thought to do so." He dug a claw into the tender skin just under her chin, forcing her to lift her head. "They're almost in range," he murmured. "Tick tock, Serena."

"I... I can't just—"

"As a bonus to celebrate our new relationship, I'll even throw in the rescue of Zinnia Ann Turner. She was on staff at the hospital, and is imprisoned in a tiny cave just ahead. In fact, Mitchell is almost on top of her."

"What? Why is she there?"

"They took her to provide medical care, although I fail to see how a Doctors Without Borders midwife is going to help them unless they can suddenly give birth." He let go of her chin, allowing her to step back. "She's unmarried, and an appropriate age. She and Mitchell would suit, considering they both have that unfortunate hero complex."

"Is she… unharmed?"

"So far, yes, but I doubt that will remain true forever." He glanced over her head and smirked. "Did I just hear the sound of a gun being cocked?"

Letting out a breath, Serena sank to her knees for the first time in her life.

Are you on the edge of your seat? I am! Zinnia's Solstice Daddy is available wherever ebooks are sold.

For sneak peeks and teasers, sign up for my newsletter. You'll also get a free book delivered right to your inbox!

ACKNOWLEDGMENTS

As always, my undying gratitude and love go to Engineer Hubby. Without your support and faith, I wouldn't be writing at all. Love you to the moon and back, baby.

Want to see what I'm up to next? Join my Renegades on Facebook. You can also sign up for my newsletter to receive a free short story delivered right to your inbox!

facebook.com/AuthorRaisaGreywood

instagram.com/raisagreywood

bookbub.com/authors/raisa-greywood

goodreads.com/raisa_greywood

tiktok.com/@raisagreywood

Leave Me Breathless

Breaking Donatella

Bridgewater Brides

Their Wanted Bride

Cocky Hero Club

Sexy Scoundrel

Standalone Titles & Anthologies

Ladder 54: Five Firefighter Romances

Masters of the Castle: Witness Protection Program

Happily Never After (written with Sinistre Ange)

Demon Lust

Blood Lust

WICKED TRUTH - MINETTE MOREAU

SNEAK PEEK

*T*here was a problem with barricading one's door. When her maid knocked, Lily had to get up and remove the obstacle before the woman could enter without causing a commotion.

"A moment, please, Margaret! I'll be right there!"

"Yes, ma'am. A gentleman has come to call. He says his name is Duke Denforth."

Lily tied the sash of her dressing gown and removed the barricade from the door before opening it. "Did he say what he wanted?"

Whilst Lily rarely asked for her services as a lady's maid, Margaret went straight to Lily's wardrobe, choosing the best of her day dresses. "No, ma'am. He asked to speak with your mother as well. I will try to make her presentable after I dress you."

Lily allowed Margaret to take her dressing gown and assist her into her corset and pink frock. "I don't know him. And the Denforth estate is quite a distance away, if I recall." She bit her lip, wincing when her teeth caught the edge of the scabbed cut Caine had given her. "I don't understand why a duke would call on me."

"I'm sure I don't know, ma'am. Let me do something with your hair before I tend to Mrs. Archer."

"Of course." Lily sat while Margaret brushed her hair, the blonde tresses falling to her waist in a wavy curtain. With deft movements, Margaret soon had the mass pinned into an elegant chignon. Lily's belly growled, and she laid a hand over her abdomen, knowing there would be no time for breakfast while a bloody duke sat in their parlor.

She'd forgotten her stockings, but had no time to bother with them. One didn't keep a duke waiting. Hoping he wouldn't notice, Lily settled for slippers, donning them as Margaret hurried away. Taking a deep breath, she wiped her sweaty palms on her dress and went downstairs.

As she entered the parlor, Jason Martin stood and drew her into his arms. Kissing her cheek, he said, "It's good to see you again. You look beautiful, Lily."

She grinned and hugged him tightly, so glad to see her oldest friend, aside from Elizabeth. "What are you doing here? I thought you were apprenticed to—"

"I came back to see to my brothers and met these gentlemen. They wish to make your acquaintance." Laying a hand on her arm, he kissed her once more and backed away.

A man in a somber gray suit turned away from the window to face her, and she realized he must be Duke Denforth. He looked vaguely familiar, but she couldn't place where she'd seen him. His brown hair was untidy, as if he'd been outside in a gale. His nose was straight and perfect over full lips, and his jaw had just a hint of reddish stubble. He smiled at her, flashing straight, white teeth. He wasn't particularly tall, but his carriage and bulk under the fine wool of his coat lent him quite an imposing appearance.

Two men stood with him; one dark as a midnight sky, and the other fair, with the pale complexion and red hair of an Irishman. Men with dark skin were uncommon in the countryside, and she tried to hide her avid perusal of him. The dark man's bald head and a livid scar across one cheek kept him from being conventionally handsome, but he was the most striking man she'd ever seen. Truly, both Duke

Denforth's servants were arresting. The redhead appeared very young until one looked into his blue eyes. They were ancient, hard, and very cool as he caught her peeking.

Both were dressed well in bespoke suits and white shirts. They were most likely Duke Denforth's servants, and she wondered why he'd brought them to meet her.

Yet it was Denforth's eyes that caught most of her attention. She'd never seen such a startling hue before. Pale almost to translucence, the green was otherworldly. She saw dew freshened leaves in his gaze, or perhaps new spring grass. Those eyes held such wisdom, and a bit of mischief.

She dropped into a curtsy, nearly forgetting her manners. "I am very sorry to keep you waiting, Your Grace. Will you all sit? Our maid will be in with tea and scones shortly."

"Don't apologize, please. It is very early, and we have arrived unannounced. It is I who should be giving you an apology."

"Dukes don't apologize." She slapped a hand over her mouth as the redhead snorted out a laugh and her face grew hot. "I do beg your pardon. I have no idea what came over me to say such an impolite thing." Despite her embarrassment, Denforth's laughter charmed her and she smiled as he bowed, then helped her to the low chaise longue. "Will you introduce me to your companions?" she asked.

"Of course, Miss Archer." Pointing first at the mahogany-skinned man, he said, "The bald one is Moses, and the redhead who looks like he's sucked on a lemon is Liam."

They each bowed in turn, making her wonder if they were indeed servants. Both men greeted her with the clipped, modulated speech of educated gentlemen. Moses had an unfamiliar, yet charming accent. Truly, it seemed they had more appropriate manners than their master. She had better sense than to chide Duke Denforth for his poor introduction.

He settled his large body rather too close to her. She relaxed, knowing no impropriety could occur with the parlor door open and Jason in attendance. The situation was so disconcerting. Lily had no idea why he would visit her, nor did she remember ever meeting him. Why, such a man shouldn't have known of her existence, much less visited at such an unseemly hour.

Knowing she had a very short time before her mother appeared, she gathered her nerve and asked, "Why have you come to call on me, Your Grace?"

He smiled softly, his eyes considering and thoughtful. "I will discuss it when your mother arrives. I am led to believe you don't have a male relative, so it is her to whom I will direct my inquiry."

"Yes, Your Grace. My father passed away some time ago." Lily could think of only one reason a man might make such a statement, but couldn't fathom why a duke would ask for the hand of a ruined girl with no title and a miniscule dowry, not to mention the fact that the banns had already been read for her marriage to Caine. As her friend Elizabeth had once said, marriage often involved men of middle age with bad breath and worse habits. All of those things were true of Caine Martin.

Settling back against the cushions, she hid a sigh. Duke Denforth's visit must have something to do with her late father's work. Papa had been a gifted scholar of plants and natural remedies for illness. Many of his experiments still grew in the kitchen garden and in the tiny greenhouse abutting the garden wall. Duke Denforth surely meant to purchase plants, or perhaps one of her father's books.

Truly, she was disappointed that she'd found a reasonable explanation for Denforth's presence.

She'd quite liked the idea of a young and attractive duke rescuing her from the distressing fate awaiting her. She looked down at her work-worn hands and short nails. Those fanciful tales never came true except in stories, although Elizabeth seemed happy enough with her handsome earl.

When her mother tottered into the room, leaning heavily on Margaret's arm, Duke Denforth stood and helped her into the overstuffed chair in front of the fire.

Dropping a short curtsy, Margaret said, "I'll return with tea in a moment."

When the door shut behind her, Duke Denforth turned to Lily's mother, and said, "Thank you for accepting my call so early in the morning. I'm sorry to disturb you, but there is a matter I wish to discuss."

"I can't imagine what interest we would hold for you, Your Grace. My late husband had very few debts, and I'm sure they've been paid off." Grimacing, she adjusted the black scarf covering her gray hair. "Did Mr. Archer owe money to you? He did nothing aside from putter in that abysmal garden of his. He kept us fed with his tinctures, I suppose."

"No, he didn't. May I also add my condolences for your loss." He knelt in front of her chair. "I wish to contract a marriage with your daughter, Lily Archer."

Her mother barked out a laugh, sounding much like a hyena Lily had once seen at the zoo in London. "She's already engaged to the innkeeper. Besides, she's ruined for a decent marriage. As much as I love my daughter, I'm afraid that's the best she's likely to get."

"You would sentence her to a loveless marriage with a man who hits her?"

"She would have better choices had she not..." Lily's mother sighed and dabbed at her eyes with a handkerchief. "I'm afraid the matter is already done, Your Grace. She will be married to Caine Martin next week. It will be a fitting fate for a girl with loose morals."

Lily squeezed her eyes shut to stifle her tears at her mother's words, humiliated beyond anything she'd ever experienced. She'd thought her mother loved her, but Abigail Archer planned to force the marriage to punish Lily for something she hadn't done. She supposed she'd known it, but the proof of her mother's feelings toward her made her heart ache. Was she so unworthy of love and respect that even her own mother believed her to be either losing her wits or a whore? And to say such things in front of guests sent a wave of sick shame through her stomach.

Once again, she wished she'd stood up for herself all those months ago, but looking at her mother's judgmental face, she didn't think it would have helped. To her surprise, Moses and Liam moved to stand behind her, each resting a hand on her shoulders. The gesture was more comforting than she'd expected, and she wondered at their sudden attentiveness.

Duke Denforth got up and shook his head. "I'm afraid you're wrong about that, Mrs. Archer."

"I beg your pardon?"

"I am the man who was in Lily's bedchamber that night. I can also tell you that Lily is as chaste and pure as the day she was born." Turning to Lily, he added, "Even if she's been indiscreet with someone else, which I highly doubt, I don't care. Furthermore, I have enough money and power to prevent that farce of a wedding you have planned."

Her mother's face turned purple with rage and she sputtered. "You have no right to say such things to me! I am Lily's mother, and—"

Duke Denforth held up his hand, cutting off her words. "Someone should have said them to you. Do you not see the bruises on your daughter? What happened to a mother being a safe haven for her child?"

He tossed a piece of parchment into Lily's mother's lap. "The contract with Caine Martin is dissolved, and I have a special license signed by the bishop. Miss Archer will not suffer from abuse, or your vile innuendo any longer. You may keep her damned dowry, and I'll throw in another twenty thousand to cheer your wicked soul."

Lily stood, unsure of what she intended to do. She'd always wished to see the man who had violated her so thoroughly without ever touching her, and she considered the words she'd wanted to give him.

"Excuse me."

Duke Denforth continued to trade barbs with her mother, but Lily was done listening. She got between them, facing him. "I said, shut your bloody mouths!"

She ought to be ashamed of her appalling language. It had come out almost without her control. Her angry screech brought dead, blessed silence, and she took a deep breath before addressing the rake in front of her. Margaret stood at the door to the parlor, her mouth open in shock as she wisely made herself scarce. Jason sat in his corner, a large grin on his face as he waved an encouraging hand in her direction.

"Did you just say you were the man in my room?" Lily asked.

"Yes, my dear, I will—"

"And you admit in front of witnesses that you didn't touch me?"

Taking her hand, he rubbed her knuckles. "I never laid a hand on you! Please, let me apologize—"

She pulled her hand away. "You let me suffer ruin. You let me get engaged to that foul innkeeper, and you let me debase myself entertaining Caine's filthy customers. Why do you come forth now?"

"I will explain everything after we are—"

Something energized her, a glancing touch of power that coursed through her veins. She tried to grasp it, but the energy escaped her, and she was too furious to chase it. With a scream of rage, she balled up her fist and planted a facer right to Denforth's nose.

Blood spurted and she backed away before facing her mother. "If he's still here when I return, I will accept Duke Denforth's proposal. We will be married as soon as he cleans up his face, and I will make his life a living hell for the next three hundred and thirty-two days." She stomped her foot and shook out her sore hand. "That is the precise amount of time I have suffered from his carelessness."

Both of Denforth's companions looked as if they were about to burst into laughter, and it made her even more furious, if that was possible. She pushed past them and called for Margaret to fetch Father Reynolds, then went to the kitchen to eat one of Margaret's delicious scones and swallow down a cup of tea.

She shouldn't have punched Duke Denforth. She'd been sorry for it the moment the blood gushed from his nose. And she truly didn't mean to be a shrew. He'd tried to apologize, but she'd been so angry, it was as if something had taken over her voice, making her say all those ugly words without her permission.

Guilt plagued her for her thoughts, but Lily no longer cared about her mother's opinions. It hurt that her mother thought so badly of her when she'd never done a single thing to invite her judgment. It was most likely true she would have gotten no better offer, but that didn't excuse her mother's behavior. What mother purposely pushed her only child into an abusive marriage? Even if she had done what the townspeople accused her of, there was no excuse for such treachery. Why, her mother had even said she should share Caine's bed before their wedding!

As if she would ever do such a thing. She took a deep breath to calm herself and said a prayer of thanks that her father wasn't alive to witness her mother's behavior. He'd been such a kind and gentle soul, and would be horrified by the situation. The thoughts brought a pang of sorrow. Her father would have believed her. He would have protected her.

To her surprise, Jason followed her into the kitchen and poured their tea while she fussed with the plate of scones. Setting jam and cream on the table, she asked, "Did you come to see my humiliation so you could tell your father?"

A flash of hurt darkened his brown eyes. "I followed to make sure you were all right. My father will never trouble you again," Jason replied. "I think between me and your husband-to-be, we've convinced him of the error of his ways."

She felt horrible for her unkind words. Jason wouldn't do such a thing. Laying her hand atop his, she said, "I'm sorry I said that. It was an awful thing to say. But what makes you think I should marry Denforth? By his own admission, he—"

"Came back when you needed him most, Lily."

Ignoring the scones and tea, he squeezed her hand. "He's bought a special license, and left my father in a bleeding heap for you."

"I rather think you did that."

"No, I started it. Duke Denforth finished." Shuddering, he added, "I don't know that I'd have gone that far, but perhaps my father has learned his lesson."

Lily split a scone and spread jam on it. Her appetite had fled, despite her earlier hunger. "I've already said I'll marry him. I suppose we'll just have to wait and see if he stays for the wedding."

"He'll be there when you're ready," Jason said.

Why was Jason so sure of that? She couldn't join him in his faith. But perhaps being known as a termagant would be better than being known as a whore. At least this time, she'd have done what people accused her of.

MYRDDIN WIPED the blood from his face. He ignored the shrieking woman in the chair, and grinned. What a magnificent creature his Lily was! Untaught, she'd pulled a thread of his magic away, keeping it for her own to give her enough strength to punch him. And she'd done a bloody fine job of it, to boot.

He held his handkerchief to his face and surreptitiously pushed his broken nose back into place, using a touch of magic to heal the break as Moses and Liam tried to hold back their laughter. Fates, it had been centuries since he'd seen such a powerful familiar. It was no wonder Angeline had wanted her.

"...and I cannot believe my daughter struck you! I swear to you, we brought her up better than that!"

"Do be quiet, Mrs. Archer. I deserve Lily's wrath, but she's given me a bit of a headache."

The older woman scowled, but held her peace. He thanked the heavens for small blessings as he, Moses, and Liam walked outside to wait for his bride to return.

When the door shut behind them, Liam let his laughter burst forth. "I shouldn't laugh, old friend, but the look on your face when that tiny girl punched you..." He sputtered and snorted, his giggles increasing until he had to lean against the side of the house.

"It was a surprise, to be sure," he murmured.

"You're not upset?" Moses asked, looking at him speculatively.

"No, I quite deserved her abuse." He sniffed and

rubbed at his sore nose. "Although it is my hope she will keep her fists to herself after we marry."

Nodding, Moses said, "She seems a dutiful and obedient girl under normal circumstances." Wrinkling his nose, he added, "I didn't expect her to have such a sweet disposition, given her mother's appalling behavior."

When he got his laughter under control, Liam said, "I like her. She has pretty manners, and it was a delight to see her give you your comeuppance."

Myrddin sighed and shook his head. Truly, he'd been shocked at Lily's obviously uncharacteristic fit of temper. Rather than making him leery of marrying her, it only made him more intent upon having her as his wife. Despite her softness, he saw an iron will under the façade of a pale English rose. "We have something to attend to while we wait for my bride to get ready," he said.

"Oh?" Moses asked. "We'll stand with you, and you've got a ring for her. What else do we need?"

"We need to investigate her garden," Myrddin said, gesturing for them to follow as he led the way toward the blackberry bushes. "I found a nasty bit of magic in there last night that seems to siphon its health, and Lily's, too, I believe."

"Whose is it?" Liam asked, his eyes intent upon Myrddin's.

"I think it might be a stray from Angeline. She scattered magic everywhere without considering the consequences, but I didn't have time to investigate it when I was here last. Regardless," he said, walking toward the garden, "I need to make sure it's neutralized so it can't hurt anyone."

"If it was Angeline's, it will fade in good time," Moses said.

"But what if it isn't?" Liam asked.

"Once we have Lily safely in our home, I'll come back and take care of it." Yet when they reached the wall where the sick plants were, the spell had moved to another section of the garden. The plants had been pruned of blighted leaves, and when he tasted the fruit of the blackberry vine, he found it sweet. Lily's small footprints went back and forth through the beds, and he could see divots where she'd knelt to care for the injured foliage.

"The spell was here before, but now it's moved." As he pointed to the burgeoning blight on a climbing rosebush, he heard conversation from the lane and stood, cutting off his investigation when Lily's maid approached with the reverend.

He had suspicions about the nature of the foul enchantment that sickened this garden, but it didn't make sense that one of the dark Sidhe would set a spell in a place inhabited by a young woman, especially one with a small trace of light Sidhe blood. Why would the dark Sidhe bother with Lily Archer, especially when it would likely raise the ire of King Omer? King Teran of the dark Sidhe wouldn't stand for any risk to the fragile peace existing between them.

"You should ask that dragon you're carrying about," Liam whispered as the reverend walked toward the house. "He might know something."

Once Lily's maid had escorted the reverend inside, Myrddin turned to Liam. "Drako sleeps, as he has for almost a thousand years. He has no interest in conversation," Myrddin replied, unwilling to admit that he'd entertained the idea himself. However, it was always the wisest course of action to let sleeping dragons lie, even if the dragon's massive bulk rested across his shoulders.

A quietly shut door and footsteps on the gravel heralded Jason coming to join them. His lips twitched into a smile as he approached, his large hands tucked behind his back. By the time he got to the small group, he'd erased the expression from his face. But then Liam snorted, his face turning pink as he tried to hold the laughter inside.

Myrddin looked on in disgust mixed with amusement as the younger men collapsed to a marble bench next to a blooming rose bush. Leaning against each other, they laughed helplessly.

"Did you see his face?" Liam asked. "She popped his nose like a tomato!"

"We shouldn't be laughing at a duke, you know," Jason whispered.

"You're laughing, too."

"I can't help it," Jason replied, wiping his eyes with a handkerchief. "Lily is so tiny. I never realized she had it in her!" Sobering, he stood and held his hand out to Myrddin. "I believe that Lily made her displeasure quite clear, Your Grace."

"Indeed," Myrddin replied. He'd left the swelling around his nose to avoid raising suspicion. It would fade in a few hours, and he had no interest in explaining why a bloody nose had suddenly repaired itself. "She has a bit of a temper, doesn't she?"

Jason smiled fondly as he looked toward the house. "Yes," he replied. "It's astonishing because it's so rare, but when she finally explodes, it's best to get out of the way."

"I see."

Turning back to face Myrddin, his expression went flat and sober. "Her fury is nothing compared to what mine will be if I ever learn you've hurt her. I will make what we did to my father look like a Sunday stroll, and I don't give a damn if you're a duke or the Crown Prince himself."

"I have no intention of ever hurting her, Mr. Martin." Leaning closer, Myrddin asked in a soft whisper, "Did you love her that much?"

Jason shook his head. "Yes, but not as a husband should love his wife. Lily has been one of my dearest friends since childhood." He rubbed his chin and added, "Elizabeth Stratton as well, I suppose. Lily gave us both a place to hide when our parents became unmanageable."

Myrddin had no fear of the young man, of course. Despite his size, he was no match for a mage. Yet it cost him nothing to reassure Jason, and perhaps it would please his soon-to-be wife. It also gave him some insight into her character, and he wasn't unhappy with what he found. "She has a very good friend in you. I think she would be happy if you write to her, and it would be my honor to have you visit us after we're settled."

"We'll see, Your Grace." He smiled and shook his head. "I'm just a simple cooper, and I doubt I'd fit in a duke's household. But if it will please Lily, I'll visit." Glancing back at the house, his eyes lit up when he saw Lily's maid waving at them. "It looks like it's time for me to give away the bride."

Myrddin and his companions followed him back to the house. It was surprising how quickly a confirmed bachelor would jump into the parson's mousetrap for the right woman. He wondered if the young Countess Shepton would be amused by his choice. More likely, she'd be furious.

Without another word, they walked into the parlor. He stopped, his hand on the doorframe as he stared at his wife-to-be. Her honey blonde hair hung to her waist in loose curls, and was held back with ivory combs. Her blue dress was a perfect match for her spitefully glittering eyes. The capped sleeves and heart shaped bodice revealed several bruises on her pale skin, and he wanted to slit Caine Martin's throat.

Ignoring the stares and sour expressions from everyone in attendance, save himself, Liam, and Moses, he walked toward her and bowed over her hand. "I've never seen a more beautiful bride. I am honored beyond measure to call you my wife."

Will Lily forgive her handsome duke? Find out in Wicked Truth available FREE wherever ebooks are sold.

For sneak peeks and teasers, sign up for Minette's newsletter. You'll also get a free book delivered right to your inbox!